THE MOTHER-IN-LAW

KIERSTEN MODGLIN

www.kierstenmodglinauthor.com
Cover Design: Tadpole Designs
Editing: Three Owls Editing
Proofreading: My Brother's Editor
Formatting: Tadpole Designs
First Print Edition: 2020
First Electronic Edition: 2020

To my mom—for being my biggest fan from day one

PROLOGUE

I'd woken up a normal person, but I'd go to bed that night a murderer. The thought ran through my head with a vengeance. We patched up the wall in silence, working diligently side by side. Neither of us wanted to speak of what we'd done. It was too much. No one could ever know our secret.

He assured me that everything would be okay, but I didn't believe it. Couldn't. I'd never killed anyone before that day, never watched someone's light leave their eyes. I'd always believed that was some melodramatic cliché you read in books, but I'd been wrong.

There was no other way to describe the phenomenon that had occurred as their life slipped away. A dim light faded out of the dark eyes and I'd known, without checking for a pulse, that they were gone.

Now, all that was left to do was to clean up our mess and move on with our lives. I was worried, my hands shaking so hard I could barely do the job I'd been tasked with.

He placed his hand on my shoulder, his soft eyes looking down at me without judgment for all I'd done.

"You've got to toughen up," he said, his words harsh despite his soft tone. "It's done. Falling apart won't change it. If we go out there and anyone sees you looking like this, they'll suspect something's happened. Go into the restroom and clean your face. I'll finish up."

I nodded. I couldn't tell if he was scolding me or trying to offer comfort. Either way, I walked across the hardwood floor of my bedroom and into the restroom across the hall.

When I glanced in the mirror, the woman looking back at me was unrecognizable. Blood was speckled across my straw-colored hair and porcelain skin.

I stuck my hands into the sink, watching the water run red. He was right, of course. I had to pull myself together.

This day had never happened. If anyone asked, I would tell them just that.

CHAPTER ONE

LOREN

"Don't let go of my hand," I said, squeezing my daughter's tiny fingers in mine as we made it through another large crowd. I'd never seen the riverwalk so full of people. Of course the town's festival had to fall on the day we'd been gifted free family portraits. Rynlee, unaware of any danger that may befall her, zigzagged in between groups of people, pulling me along with her as quickly as our legs would go. The ice cream cone in her hand, a small bribe that was ultimately necessary to maintain her good mood, was melting down her sticky hands, and I cringed at the thought of it landing on her clothes. *Thank God for Tide pens.*

Finally, she stopped at the edge of the road. Though she was too incredibly brave, she knew the rules and, for the most part, followed them well. She looked left, then right.

There were no cars coming from either direction, so she looked up to me for permission to cross. Before I could say anything, I felt someone shove me forward, my knees buckling underneath me as my hand squeezed tighter onto hers.

We fell together onto the cobblestone street, and I felt the sting of a cut on my palm.

"Rynlee, are you okay?" I cried, pulling the girl into my arms as I forced us back up. She was sobbing, her little hands scraped raw. Her ice cream lay smashed on the pavement, and a golden yellow dog pounced around happily at our feet, his tongue lapping up the spilled treat.

Once my daughter had caught sight of the pup, her attention was lost to me, and she tried to throw herself out of my arms.

"Can I pet him?" she asked with a laugh, reaching her hand out toward the dog. I pulled her back.

"No, not while he eats. We don't know this dog," I told her. "He could be mean."

He cocked his head to the side as if I'd hurt his feelings, and I glanced down at my daughter's pants. Her white jeans were covered in filth from the street. "*Oh*, Ryn, look at your clothes." There was no way a Tide pen was taking that out. Family pictures were definitely canceled.

Before I could focus too much on the mess I'd have to clean later, I heard hurried footsteps rushing toward us. "I'm so sorry," a male voice called. "I'm *so* sorry. Did he hurt you?" I turned to see a man with medium-length brown hair, a flannel shirt, and a strong jawline rushing toward me. His eyes were filled with concern as he grabbed the leash that was connected to the dog's neck. "*Merlin*," he scolded, then looked up at me again. "I'm so sorry," he repeated. "He took off. There were some birds or something. I guess he thought he could catch them. I couldn't get through the crowd to stop him in time." He looked me up and down. "I'm really, really sorry. Is there anything I can do? Can I get you some clean clothes? Offer you some bandages?"

"We're fine," I told him, though I was incredibly disappointed our plans had been ruined. It had taken me hours to coax Rynlee into clean clothes and curl her hair.

Interrupting my thoughts, Ryn cried out, "Can I pet him?"

He smiled sheepishly, looking at me and then her. "Uh, I don't mind if your mom says it's okay."

"Will he bite?" I asked, looking at the dog with concern.

"No, Merlin's nice," he said. "Just rambunctious and especially weak around food—which I'm happy to replace." He gestured toward the smashed ice cream and patted the dog's head. "God love him, he's honestly such a good dog except for that."

"Okay," I said, setting Rynlee down carefully. She reached for his head, leaning in for a hug. She'd always loved animals, though I'd never been a fan.

"I feel *so* bad. Are you sure you don't want me to help you guys get cleaned up? I own a shop right across the way. I have a first aid kit and everything. Your hand looks...pretty bad."

His eyes trailed across my bloody palm as I held it up, trying to dry the blood with the sleeve of my sweater. "I, um, are you sure?" Suddenly, I was aware of the wound again, and I felt the sting searing through my skin, cold as ice.

"It's the least I can do," he said, pulling at the leash. "Come on, it's right this way." He pulled the leash so Merlin would back up and began leading us through the busy boardwalk.

"Hand, Rynlee," I instructed her, holding out my hand for hers.

"I wanna walk with Merlin," she said, but I raised a brow at her.

"*Hand.*"

She sulked back toward me, much to the stranger's

amusement.

"Rynlee? I've never heard that. It's cute," he said.

"It's a family thing. A play on my name. Which is Loren, by the way. My mom was Laurel, I'm Loren, this is Rynlee, Ryn for short. Loren—Ryn, " I said, bouncing my head from side to side to show how I'd gotten from my name to hers. I'd always spouted off at the mouth when I was nervous, and around this handsome stranger I apparently couldn't shut up.

"I like it," he said, obviously unfazed by my babbling. "I'm Jack, and you've already met Merlin."

I laughed. "Up close and personal."

He smiled at me, his eyes lingering on my face a bit longer than expected. "Well, hopefully we can get you patched up. I hope he didn't ruin your clothes."

I brushed a hand over my sweater. "I'm sure it'll be fine. Luckily her clothes are white, so they can be bleached. The rest should come out with pretreatment."

He nodded as he slowed in front of a building to let a group of women pass us. "My mother's in town visiting. We can ask her about how to get the stains out. She knows about all that stuff."

"Your mother?" I asked. Suddenly, I felt unsubstantiated pressure. I didn't want to meet this stranger's mother. I especially didn't want to meet this *handsome* stranger's mother while I was covered in blood and street gunk. Before I could think of a reason to resist, he opened the door to a building and ushered me inside.

"She should be right in here."

"I thought you said you owned a shop. This is a bar," I said, looking around at the long, wooden bar and tables with their chairs flipped up on top.

"A bar with a first aid kit," he said. "And we're not open yet, so it's fine." He unhooked Merlin's leash, letting the dog roam around the empty building while he rushed around to the other side of the bar and bent down to grab something underneath. He pulled a white box out, opening it to reveal a few bandages, gauze, alcohol swabs, and trial packages of antibiotic ointment. "Here we go," he said, pulling out an alcohol swab first. He handed it to me and I tore it open, swiping it across the wound as I winced. The sharp stinging sensation had me baring my teeth in a grimace.

"Rynlee, get back over here," I called when I spotted her beginning to follow Merlin across the room.

Her shoulders slumped, but she began to head my way, stopping in the middle of the room and sinking onto the floor. Jack opened a pouch of ointment and placed it on the wound with care, then tore open some gauze and wrapped it around my wrist.

I tried to pretend I wasn't incredibly sensitive to his touch by watching Rynlee sitting on the floor. The truth was, it was all I could think about. His hands moved across my skin slowly, our cells connecting with an electricity I hadn't felt in so long.

"There you go, that should do it," he said, setting my arm on the bar carefully.

"Thank you," I said. "That's much better."

"No problem," he said. "I much prefer bandaging *you* to the many, many men that I have the *dis*pleasure of bandaging at the end of a long night of drinking." He chuckled, and his laugh was surprisingly warm. It sent warm tingles across my skin, and I couldn't break his eye contact.

Finally, he looked away, using his hand to sweep the mess into the trash can under the bar. "Does she need anything?"

"Hers were mostly just scrapes," I said. "Maybe just an alcohol wipe to sanitize it?" He handed one over before closing the box.

I walked across the room to where my daughter sat with Merlin's head resting on her lap.

"He seems to like her," he said.

"Yeah," I agreed, working to get her hands clean. She winced with my every move, but her opposite hand didn't leave the dog's head. "I think she likes him, too." I wondered if it was going entirely over his head that I wasn't sure if we were only talking about Merlin and Rynlee.

When I glanced back at Jack, aware that he hadn't said anything for a moment too long, I saw him staring up across the banister that led to some unseen space at the top floor of the bar. "Is everything okay?" I asked, drawing his attention back to me.

"S-sorry," he said, shaking his head to apparently clear his thoughts. "I was just looking for my mom. I'm not sure where she's gone off to."

"Right. Your mom." I had almost forgotten.

"Anyway," he said, letting out a breath and rendering his mouth into a smile. "It doesn't matter. She's around here somewhere."

"Does she live here?" I pointed up to where he'd been staring.

"No," he said. "She lives in Herrinville. She's just here visiting for the week."

"Oh, that's nice," I said, letting out a small sigh of relief.

"We're very close," he told me. Then, noticing what must've been a strange expression on my face, he asked, "Is that weird?"

I shook my head. "My mother died a few years ago. We

used to be close, too. So, I think it's nice to have her around. I hope Rynlee doesn't kick me to the curb first chance she gets," I said, glancing down. Rynlee was standing up next to me, but still refused to draw her attention from her new canine companion.

"That's why I have a dog," he jested. "They never leave you."

"Except when they're plowing down strangers in the streets, you mean?"

"Hey, what can I say? My dog has good taste." He winked as he said it, though I was sure it wasn't my imagination that his face had gone a darker shade of red. I let out a small laugh, but there was a knot in my stomach that was making it hard to form proper thoughts.

"Well, thank you," I said finally, lifting my hand with my daughter's in it. "For helping us."

"It was the least I could do, like I said, after I caused you to need the help."

"Well, it wasn't all your fault," I said, "but it seems the culprit is the most forgiven. I'm going to have to drag her away from him."

"You're welcome to stay," he said. "For lunch. I was just about to grab a bite. I owe you a replacement ice cream cone anyway."

"Oh, that's kind of you, but we should really get home and change. We've got to meet my cousin for dinner in a few hours."

"Oh. Well, that's all right," he said, trying to keep a smile on his face, though I could read the disappointment from where I stood across the room.

"But maybe some other time?"

He perked his head up. "I'd like that."

"I—I didn't catch your last name, Jack," I said, my statement more of a question.

"Jack Wells," he told me, holding out his hand. I stepped forward to shake it, and the same electricity was there the moment our skin collided.

"It was really nice to meet you, Jack Wells. I'm Loren Heinz, like the ketchup." I kicked myself as soon as I said it, unsure why I'd tried to be funny. Comedy was never my forte.

"My favorite brand," he said with an awkward laugh that made me feel slightly better.

"Well, we'd better go," I said. "Come on, Ryn." My daughter latched onto the dog for dear life, as if I were ripping her away from her most prized possession.

"I don't wanna go, Mom," she said. "I want to stay."

"I know, baby, but Meredith's going to be waiting for us. We have to go. We can come back some other time," I said.

"No!" She fought, wriggling in my arms until I was forced to pick her up.

"Come back anytime. You know where to find us," Jack said, watching me drag my child out the door. I smiled at him, trying my best not to look like a crazed mother, though I knew I did.

I never thought I'd see Jack again. We hadn't exchanged phone numbers and I hadn't told him about the odd spelling of my first name, so there was little chance of him finding me. It was better that way, I guessed. I didn't need to get involved with someone new, not after Rynlee's father and I had such a terrible breakup. I'd sworn off men at that point, not wanting to get myself in any more trouble.

I had no idea *just* how much trouble meeting Jack Wells would cause.

CHAPTER TWO

LOREN

M uch to my surprise, I did see Jack again—just two short weeks later. It took a few seconds for me to realize who he was as he walked into the boutique Meredith and I owned.

"Welcome," Meredith said casually over her shoulder, working on a flower arrangement in the back corner of the building.

I glanced up from where I stood at the register, taking in his appearance with confusion. It couldn't be real, he couldn't be there, and yet, he was. I watched as he walked into the shop, his eyes searching around, landing on Meredith first and finally, me.

"Hi," he said, his expression confused at first and then shocked. "Loren?" he asked.

I nodded. "Jack." His name was a whispered statement, the only word I could muster.

"I-I-can't believe it. You work here?"

"I own it," I said, my eyes darting proudly around the

room we'd put our hearts and souls into for months before opening.

"*We* own it," Meredith said playfully, bounding up to the front of the shop to see what was going on.

"Right," I agreed. "We own it. Jack, this is my cousin, Meredith."

Meredith held her hand out, smiling slyly, and I wondered what had gotten up her sleeve. "Nice to meet you, Jack." She paused. "Have we met before?"

He stared at her for a moment, but shook his head. "I don't think so."

"You look incredibly familiar." I groaned internally. Meredith was beautiful—despite being a decade older than me, she had no trouble landing guys my age and even younger. It hadn't bothered me before, not really, because I'd basically sworn off guys since Travis, but I couldn't help finding her abrasive personality particularly overwhelming in this scenario. "How do you know Loren?"

"We met in Oakton a few weeks ago. Jack owns a bar downtown," I explained, my eyes widening at her. I'd talked about Jack for days after we met, so she knew all about him. I hoped she'd catch on quickly.

"Oh, he's the one that nearly trampled you?" she asked with a laugh. I watched her take a step back from him, a clear sign that she realized he wasn't hers to claim.

"Well, that was my dog, actually," he said, rubbing a hand over the back of his neck as his cheeks pinkened. "You talked about me?"

"Darling, she never stopped," she said, winking at me. "I'll leave you two to it. It was nice to meet you."

Jack shook her hand as she held it out again. Once she

was in the back of the room, he leaned in, his voice lowered. "I have a confession."

"What's that?" *He's slept with Meredith.*

His smile was small and filled with uncertainty. "I knew you worked here."

That hadn't been what I expected him to say. "You did?"

"I may have looked you up," he said. "But I didn't want to seem like a crazy stalker, so I waited a while to come in. And…well, it still felt a little crazy, but I wanted to see you and—"

I put my hand across the counter to where his lay, just for a moment. "I'm glad you came."

Relief filled his expression. "Really?"

"Mhm, very much so. I forgot your last name by the time I'd made it home the day we met, and I couldn't very well come back into the bar without making it obvious that's why I'd come. I was…I mean, I didn't know if you—"

"I do," he said, and it was his turn to place his hand over mine.

"You do?"

He nodded. "I like you, Loren." His brows raised with assurance. "A lot."

I smiled, my cheeks warming. I'd lost sight of Meredith in the store, but I knew wherever she was, she was listening with a devilish grin. "I like you, too," I admitted. "What I know about you, anyway."

"Would you like to get to know me better?" he asked. "Maybe tonight? Dinner?"

"A date?" I asked. I hadn't been asked out on a date in years, hadn't accepted in even longer.

"If that's okay with you."

I thought for a moment. I'd promised myself I'd stay away from men until Rynlee was old enough to understand. When her dad left, the pain of his betrayal had devastated her. There were still nights she cried over him, asking why he didn't want to see her. I didn't want to put her through anything like that again, so no matter what I wanted, I had to be careful of her heart. I'd promised myself that my next relationship would be the one to stick, and I couldn't give that chance to just anyone. "I...I have a daughter."

His smile disappeared for a half-second. "I know," he said simply. "I met her, remember?"

"Yes, I know, I just...I have to be careful where she's involved. Her father and I, when we split, it was insanely hard on Ryn. I can't put her through anything like that again."

"I understand," he said, his voice calm. "Really, I do. I don't want either of you to get hurt." He let go of my hand and stepped back.

"I'm sorry," I said.

"No worries. Just...if you change your mind, you know where to find me." He turned to walk away, but stopped. My heart leapt with unexpected hope when he began to speak again. "Oh, I forgot. It's probably too late by now, but my mom said peroxide and dish soap should get those stains out."

I smiled at him, feeling unexpected tears in my eyes. It was silly, and I couldn't explain why they'd come on so quickly, but there they were, blurring my eyes. I guess the reason was simple: *he'd remembered.* He'd remembered my stain, remembered me. Travis was never the thoughtful type, never one to remember anniversaries or even birthdays half the time. He certainly never remembered little details, like the fact that I preferred dark to milk chocolate, or white to red wine. Once, he even forgot I was allergic to scented fabric softener. I had a rash for days after he'd washed a load in Hawaiian Breeze. "Thank you." As he turned around again with a slight nod, I sucked in a deep breath, beginning to speak.

Before I could utter a word, he'd spun back to face me with eyes full of hope. "Yeah?"

"If we did go out, we'd have to take things slow."

"That's no problem. In fact, I prefer it that way. Merlin gets attached too easily."

I pressed my lips together, shaking my head dotingly at him, my cheeks pink from happiness. "When would you like to go?"

"Is tonight too fast for you?"

I studied his face, the lines of wisdom and laughter, the dark eyes that met mine with a sort of deep connection I hadn't experienced in so long. There was kindness there, a kindness that ran deep, and a childlike quality—playfulness, that would make for a wonderful quality in a partner and a father for Rynlee someday.

I was getting ahead of myself, I knew, but Jack was like that. He made me see a future. Believe in a future again. He seemed to be everything Travis wasn't—caring, because he'd patched up my arm, thoughtful, because he'd remembered to ask his mom about the stain Merlin caused, and attentive, because he'd searched me out. I had been the one to ask Travis out the first time, the one to call him back after a week of not hearing anything after that date. I'd pushed too hard, according to Meredith. Done too much. He was the one supposed to woo me, but I'd just liked him *so* much. With Jack, it felt right. I stayed still and he chased. This was how it should be. He was everything I needed. So far, anyway. I needed to slow down, for Rynlee's sake if nothing else.

Instead, I heard myself saying, "Tonight's perfect."

CHAPTER THREE

LOREN

"Are you sure I look okay?" I asked, staring at the mirror and picking apart my every flaw. It wasn't like me to put so much concern into how I looked. I spent much more time on Rynlee's appearance than my own, but I wanted to look nice that night. I think Meredith could tell, because she stood and walked toward me, smoothing down my hair and kissing my head.

Since my mother had died, Meredith had become like a stand-in mom for me, our twelve-year age difference enough that most of the time she felt more like a parent than a friend. On top of that, she had more memories of my mom than I did, and it comforted me to learn about her.

"You look beautiful. He won't know what hit him." She bumped my hip playfully with hers. "You're just missing one thing." She reached for the bed where her purse lay—it was blue with purple stitching, one of her favorites. Meredith had always made her own purses, eccentric and whimsical, just like her. She pulled out a plum lipstick, swiping it over my lips. "There, now it's perfect."

"Thanks, Mer. And you're sure you're okay to keep Rynlee?"

"Of course," she said, slapping her thigh as my daughter bounded from the bed and into her arms. "We're going to have so much fun aren't we, *Rynnee-Ren?*"

My daughter squealed with delight as Meredith spun around the room with her in her arms. They stopped spinning as the doorbell rang and my blood turned to ice in my veins. "Maybe this is too much," I said, my throat suddenly dry. "Maybe I should just wait a while. I mean, Travis and I just broke up seven months ago."

"Yeah, and good riddance to that," Meredith covered Rynlee's ears, before mouthing *'asshole.'* "He didn't deserve you, Loren, but more than that, you didn't deserve him. You deserve to be happy." She kissed Ryn's head. "Doesn't she, sweet girl? Doesn't Mommy deserve to be happy?"

"Yeah!" she screamed, throwing her arms in the air.

"But what if it's too much?"

"You won't know that if you don't get out there and try. Come on, you can do this," she said, taking my hand in hers. She pulled open the bedroom door and practically shoved me out first. "Don't keep him waiting too long. Prince Charming turns into a pumpkin at midnight."

"That's not right, Aunt Mer," Rynlee said, giggling with delight.

"It's not, huh? I thought you were on my side," she teased as we descended the oak staircase. I could see his outline through the beveled glass of my large front door.

"Here goes nothing," I said, taking a deep breath. I leaned down, kissing Rynlee's lips and pulling Meredith into a one-armed hug.

"Knock 'em dead, kiddo," she said, hugging me back before turning with Rynlee to head toward the kitchen.

"What's that mean? Knock *who* dead?" Rynlee inquired.

I didn't hear Meredith's answer as I pulled open the door. He was dressed in a black dress shirt and jeans, a bouquet of flowers in his hand. I smiled at him, glad I'd chosen to wear the dressier of my two options since we hadn't said where we were going. I ran a hand over my plum-colored dress.

"Wow," he said, swallowing visibly. "You look incredible."

"Thank you," I said. "You do too."

"Thanks." He handed me the bouquet. "I hope you like lilies. I called your store, and *Becky*, I think it was, she said she thought they were your favorite."

"I do love them," I said, and it was true. Becky was almost right. After sunflowers, they were my second favorite flower, and the bouquet he'd chosen was truly beautiful. "That was really kind of you." I placed my nose to them, breathing in their scent before setting the flowers in an empty vase on a table near me. "Come on in. Let me go get some water for these, and I'll be right back."

"It was no trouble," he said with a nod, stepping through the threshold. "I didn't want to get anything wrong." I smiled at him, trying to pretend the gesture wasn't enough to make me teary-eyed again as I compared him to my ex. He continued to amaze me. I disappeared into the kitchen, waving to Meredith who gave me a doe-eyed expression about the flowers. I rolled my eyes at her, playing off how sweet the gesture was, and ran water into the vase.

When I came back into the foyer, placing the flowers back onto the table, Jack was staring around the room in awe. "This place is really something," he said.

"Thank you. It's a family home. Passed down through the

generations, you know? I could never afford something like this in today's market."

"Well, it's incredible. I love old houses like this. My parents own one similar, but definitely not this grand."

I smiled. Truth was, my house—once called a manor—really was something special, but growing up in it, I'd never appreciated it like I supposed I should. Anytime I had guests, they always seemed to be in awe of a place that I only saw as a messy work-in-progress. There was so much I wanted to update. It made me feel a bit guilty. "You ready to go?"

"Yeah, yep." Seeming to realize he'd been too focused on the house and not enough on his date, he stepped back, holding the door open for me.

"So, where are you taking me?"

WE ARRIVED at the restaurant a half hour later. It was a quiet steakhouse I'd seen a thousand times but never bothered to stop at.

"Do you like Able's?" he asked, nodding his head toward the restaurant as he unbuckled his seatbelt and climbed from the car.

"I wouldn't know. I've never eaten here," I said, joining him on the sidewalk.

"You haven't?" He folded his arm, holding out his elbow for me to loop my arm through. "Oh, it's one of my favorite places. It's understated, you know? It doesn't have the attitude of a five-star, but I swear the food's every bit as good if not better."

I smiled as he let go of my arm to open the door for me. "Well, don't make me take your word for it."

"I don't plan on it," he said joyfully, rushing forward to get the interior door.

We walked into the crowded room, the smell of simmering steak and onions hitting my nose all at once. It was warm, comfortably so, and a smiling waiter approached us within seconds of entering. "Hello, table for two?"

I nodded and the waiter grabbed two menus from a stack at the edge of a table and took a few steps, indicating where to follow. Jack held his arm out so I would go in front of him. His hand touched the small of my back to let me know he was there. I didn't need him to do it, but I found comfort in the fact that he did. My ex was very distant, and he rarely touched me unless he wanted something. To feel another human's touch is a very intimate thing, I've found. It's why we shy away from touching knees with strangers when we're in close proximity to them. It's why holding hands is such a big deal. Because touch, more than a kiss and more than sex, is the single thing that connects us as humans. At least, that's what I've always believed.

We were led to a table in the far corner of the room and the waiter set our menus down, took our drink orders, then scurried away. Before we'd even begun talking, Jack's phone rang. "I'm sorry about this," he said, pulling it from his pocket. His face grew serious as he stood. "I'm...really sorry. I have to take this. I'll be right back."

I swallowed, trying not to feel bitter as he darted away from the table and out of the restaurant. Didn't people usually wait until the date had gone poorly to fake an emergency? Was I really so bad at this? Had I already frightened him away? I looked around the crowded room, trying not to appear as pitiful as I felt. I met another woman's eyes—she was clearly on a date herself—and when she looked away too fast, I knew she'd seen what had happened. Embarrassment radiated through me, and I felt my cheeks growing too hot. I considered my options, wondering how long was too long to stay and wait? Would he bother to explain himself? Should I at least pay for our drinks before darting? I watched the door with hopeful eyes, each moment that passed more painful than the one before it. When I was ready to give up, I let out a heavy breath, spying him hurrying back into the building.

"I'm sorry," he said, sitting down across from me once again.

I tried not to look as relieved as I felt. "It's okay."

"No, it's not," he said. "I know it's not. I sincerely apologize, Loren. It was my mother. I wouldn't have picked up for anyone else."

"Is...everything all right?"

"She was calling to check in, but I wanted to be sure it wasn't anything too serious. I'll talk to her later, though, and again, I'm sorry. I promise it won't happen again." He scooted further in toward the table, laying out his napkin. "So, let's get back to our date, shall we? Tell me about yourself, Loren," he said, placing his folded hands on the table and leaning toward me.

"I'm pretty boring," I said, dismissing his question rather quickly. I was just relieved he'd returned and that he hadn't taken another girl's call while he was with me, like Travis did on our second date. What was there to say that Jack didn't already know? That wouldn't scare him away?

"Somehow I doubt that's true."

"It is. Annoyingly so."

"Tell me about Rynlee, then."

Now, that was easier. I sucked in a breath. "She's...stubborn.

Full of life. She loves to play pretend and dress-up—I can barely keep her out of her costumes. She loves to dance. I'm pretty sure she danced before she could walk. Her laugh can make me laugh, even when I'm furious. She hates having her hair done, hates to get dressed. She loves chocolate and peppermint, but not together." I heaved a sigh. "Honestly, she's just the sweetest little thing. I'm not sure how I would get on without her." I was staring at the tabletop, thinking of her with blurring vision. Motherhood had made me so sappy, I cried at the drop of a hat now. I hated to be away from her, even for a moment.

"You're a good mom," he said finally.

"I try to be," I said. "But I've made mistakes."

"Who hasn't?" He shrugged.

"Do you have kids?" The waiter approached and placed our drinks in front of us. He took a sip of his wine before answering.

"No," he said. "I've never been married."

"Neither have I," I told him. "Rynlee's father and I were engaged, but we called it off a little less than a year ago."

"I'm sorry," he said, reaching out to take my hand.

"Are you?" I asked with a slight smirk.

There was that laugh again, the one that made me weak in the knees. "No, not really." He added, too quickly, "Only because that had to happen for us to be here."

"Here is pretty great," I said, looking around the room. I leaned toward him, anxious to carry on the conversation. "So, what's wrong with *you*, then? What skeletons are in your closet?"

He took another drink with raised eyebrows. "Nothing, I hope. I just...you know, haven't met the right woman. I've had a few serious relationships, but nothing ever..." He clicked his tongue. "Nothing ever stuck. What about you? Why did your engagement end?"

I took a drink, clearing my head as I prepared to answer. Whatever I said, it couldn't be the truth. "I...you know, we just wanted different things. With Rynlee especially. I wanted to settle down and build a life here, but he was still chasing dreams that he'd long since outgrown." I froze. "Not that I think there's an age limit on dreams, of course there's not. But...I had the shop, which I know it's not that big of a deal, but it was all I've ever wanted. To be my own boss." I smiled. "Co-boss. To make the decisions. It was my dream, and I had that. He always felt like he needed to have a dream, any dream, to compete. He wanted to be in music, to produce or play in a band, but he had, *this is going to sound terrible*, but he had no drive. He didn't want to work for any of it. He'd get so frustrated with me, because my dream had come *easy*—his words, not mine. Why did I get to live my dream when he couldn't? So, eventually, I just realized what he needed and it wasn't me. Or us. He left seven months ago, and we haven't heard from him since."

I traced my finger across the lip of my glass, staring at my reflection in the crimson of my wine.

"I'm so sorry, Loren," he said, seemingly at a loss for words.

"Oh," I looked up, waving off his concerns, "no, don't be. I mean, yeah, it sucked at the time, but I'm fine. Honestly. Rynlee is all that I care about, and I have the shop to provide for us financially and keep me busy, so it's all good. I just... you know, I don't want to scare you off, but I've promised myself that the next time I get serious with someone, it has to stick. I can't risk her getting hurt again."

He pressed his lips together. "Or yourself getting hurt again?"

I gave a stiff nod, looking away. "Rynlee's the most important part of it, but yes. I'd rather not get hurt if I can avoid it. Meredith says I tend to...fall fast."

"It must get lonely," he said. "Parenting alone. I have such respect for single parents."

"Well, we all get lonely sometimes," I said. I desperately wanted to change the subject. "I'm sure you understand that."

"I do, more than you know." It was refreshing how honest he was with me. There was no attempt to hide himself from me or pretend to be stronger or cooler than he was like so many people try to do. "So, Meredith, your cousin and business partner. You must be pretty close."

I paused, wondering how to explain our relationship. "We...are."

"You hesitated." He cocked his head to the side, an amused grin spreading to his lips.

"We're close," I insisted, "it's just...complicated."

"Complicated how?"

"Well, Meredith is quite a bit older than me, but she's the only family I have left. We grew up with her kind of playing my older sister, and eventually falling into a sort of motherly role, I guess. Her daughter's just a few years younger than me, but I always had more in common with Meredith than Dora."

"Her daughter?"

"Mhm." I took a sip of my moscato before continuing. "Yeah, Dora turned eighteen two years ago, and when she did...Meredith kind of, I don't know, she...had an early mid-life crisis, I guess."

"What she bought a Harley, hit the road?"

"No, but she probably *dated* a Harley or two and hit the road." He laughed at my joke, which sent warmth through my body, settling in my stomach. "Her ex, Dora's father, ran off before Dora was born, and Meredith kind of swore off men while she raised her daughter. She was really hurt by it all. But when Dora moved away to college, Meredith, it was almost like she went back to who she was before Dora was born. She started dating men, she'd disappear for days and weeks at a time, go to other cities. She even left the country once with a man. She's...God love her, she's the closest family I have and I consider her one of my best friends, but sometimes it feels like I'm the parent in our relationship."

"That must get hard, running a business together."

"It does," I agreed, drawing up one corner of my lips. "But, it's not so bad. When she's there, Meredith's great. She has all these new ideas for the shop. She designs these purses that we sell, and she decided we should start making some desserts, which have done really well. She wants to start making clothes next. So, I can't complain. Her creativity is what kept our little florist shop from caving in before it began. When she's with me, she's great. She helps with Rynlee and the store. But...when she meets a guy, a guy she likes, it's...game over, sometimes." I pause, recalling the last time she'd disappeared. She called me from Miami to tell me she was going to live on a commune for a few months with a man named Dominic. I shook the memory away. "But, she's family. And I love her. What can you do?" I chuckled under my breath, wanting to change the subject. I felt guilty for talking bad about her. "So, the bar? That's pretty cool, huh?" I leaned forward. It was nice how easily we were sliding into our conversation without any of it feeling forced.

He blew air from his lips in a quiet laugh. "Yeah, it's...

well, it was my *shop*, as you said. My dream. I bought it about three years ago, and I've really tried to turn it around. You should've seen the shape it was in when I bought it."

"It really is beautiful. Did you do all the woodwork yourself?"

"I wanted it to look really rustic," he said with a nod. "So, I took a few courses. I figured it was cheaper than hiring out for it."

It hadn't escaped my attention that he'd mentioned achieving his dream shortly after I told him Travis and I hadn't worked out because he hadn't achieved his and it made him resent me. I wondered if it was to show me that he was exactly what I was looking for. My cheeks warmed from the thought.

"What are you thinking about?" he asked, leaning forward even more. He reached his hand toward mine, our skin brushing on top of the white table cloth. It was incredible how intimate our conversation felt despite the many people around us.

"Just that…you know, it's great how hard you've worked to have your dream. And you got it."

His eyes danced between mine before he answered, his expression warming as his finger ran across my palm. "Yeah, well, one small part of it, anyway."

CHAPTER FOUR

LOREN

The doorbell rang, and I nearly jumped out of my skin. Running a quick hand over my dress one last time and checking my reflection above the mantel, I ran into the foyer.

It had been eight days since I'd seen him last, on our *seventh* date, and it was enough to kill me. In the two months since I'd met Jack, it was incredible how close we'd grown. That night was important because it was the first time we'd have dinner together in my house. I'd made it clear from the beginning that I had to protect Rynlee above all else, and while Meredith was keeping her for me again that night, bringing someone else into our home felt like a huge step.

"Wow, you look incredible," he said, staring me up and down with obvious approval. I grinned, taking his hand and stepping toward the door to meet his lips.

Our kiss was like electricity, pulsing through me and making itself known at the far corners of my skin. When we pulled away, my smile was enough to make my cheeks ache. "You're not so bad yourself," I joked. "Come in." I stepped back, allowing him inside. "Excuse the mess." *Like I haven't just spent hours scrubbing every baseboard.*

"Mess?" he asked, looking up at the ceiling and around the room in awe. "This place is...*wow.*" A hand went to his mouth and he sucked in a breath. "This is really something, Loren. I mean, I know I saw some of it the night of our first date, but your home really is beautiful."

"Thanks," I said softly. "Like I told you, it was a family home. My parents', my parents' parents, their parents' parents, you know. I got it strictly because I was born."

"You're big on earning things yourself," he said. A true observation.

I nodded.

"Well, either way, you've kept it up so well. It's amazing, truly." He stepped forward, his attention no longer on the house. "Does that mean your parents are...gone? I know you mentioned your mother passing, but your father...he's gone, too?"

I nodded, the question catching me off guard. There was a raw spot in the pit of my stomach that ached every time I thought of them. Despite the fact that my mom had been gone nearly five years and my dad a decade more, it was still so hard for me to talk about them. "For a while now."

"I'm sorry," he said, and I knew he meant it. His hand found my waist and he squeezed gently, his touch warming the ice that I'd allowed to enter my body.

"It's not your fault," I said, taking his hand back in mine. "Would you like a tour before we have dinner?"

"IT'S LIKE...I mean, it's like a castle," he said when the tour had ended and we found ourselves back at the dining room table. "How do you not get lost here?"

"Meredith and I grew up playing here," I said, "so it's just second nature, I guess. It *is* huge, though. If it weren't for the long line of my family having lived here, I'd sell it in a heart-beat." At over eighty-seven-hundred square feet, my home was, by modern standards, a castle. The red house contained seven bedrooms and five bathrooms, a separate living room and den, expansive foyer, and a formal dining room separate from the oversized kitchen. Each level had enough room to be its own apartment, maybe even two. There were three stories and an attic, a large bay window that went up all three levels, and a giant and inviting, white wraparound porch. The windows had been replaced just last year, but I'd kept the majority of the exterior how it had always been, just a few fixes and updates here and there.

"You can't do that," he said, sounding offended. "People would kill for a place like this."

"I wouldn't do it. There's too much of my parents in this house, but sometimes it feels a little like I'm only working to pay an electric bill, especially in the summer with the air conditioning going."

He nodded. "Yikes, yeah I'd be scared to see what your bills look like in the summer."

"Thankfully I don't have a mortgage, because the utilities basically are one," I said with a grin. "Okay, sit. Let me get dinner on the table."

"No way," he said, reaching his hand out to stop me from walking away. "You sit. Let me serve you." He winked.

"Oooh, okay," I said in a sing-song voice, sinking into my chair so I could barely see into the kitchen when he went that way. "The casserole's in the oven, potholders are to your left there."

He followed instructions, lifting the chicken bake and carrying it carefully across the kitchen and into the dining room. He set it on the table, returning a few moments later with utensils and a bottle of wine to fill our glasses.

"You're pretty good at that. You'd think you did it for a living or something."

He rolled his eyes at me playfully. "She's got jokes, ladies and gentlemen."

I covered my mouth, laughing until my face burned red as he placed a healthy portion onto my plate. He lifted his glass as he sat, holding it out to me. "Here's to us," he said, "and to our future."

"To our future," I said, a twinkle in my eye as I began to picture it. Nights in this house with him, raising Rynlee here, maybe other children as well. I could practically see our future selves, dancing around us like ghosts in the house. It was a beautiful vision, and I couldn't let myself admit how much I hoped it would come true.

CHAPTER FIVE

LOREN

"You about ready?" I popped my head in Rynlee's bedroom and gasped. "Ryn, why did you take off your clothes?" My daughter stood, stark naked, in a room covered with toys. "And why did you get all of this out? I told you not to get too much out because Jack will be here soon."

I glanced at the Apple Watch on my wrist and sighed. He would be knocking on the door at literally any moment. Grabbing her pile of clothes from the floor, I lifted her and carried her to her bed. "Hold still," I instructed.

"I don't wanna wear this," she protested.

"Why not?"

"It's itchy," she said, wiggling her arm feverishly.

"It's not itchy, Ryn, you just wore this the other day."

"It's itchy now," she said. "I wanna wear my princess dress."

"You can't wear a costume to dinner," I said, "but if you're very good, I'll let you wear it to bed tonight."

"No, now!" she screeched, flopping down on her bed and throwing her head back.

"Rynlee, no. We don't have time for a fit." I tried to lift her, though she'd let herself become dead weight in my arms, her body like loose spaghetti as she whined through me shoving her arms into the sleeves once again.

"I don't want to wear this!" she screamed again, jerking out of my grasp.

"Fine!" I groaned, jumping as I heard the doorbell ring. "Okay, fine. You want to wear your princess dress?"

"Yes!" she said happily, clapping her hands in front of her.

"Okay," I grabbed the princess dress from her dress-up bin and tossed it over her head, pinning the cape and running my hands over the messy hair I'd meticulously combed just half an hour before. "You promise Mommy you'll be good today, right? Best behavior."

She growled in response, not giving an answer.

"Ryn?"

"I'm not Rynlee, Mommy. I'm a princess."

"Okay, well, the princess has to be on her best behavior," I told her, lifting her onto the bed and setting her down on her feet. "Come on now. We have to go." The doorbell downstairs sounded again.

"Coming!" I called down the staircase, sure he wouldn't hear me, anyway. We hurried toward the foyer, and I swung open the door in an instant. "Sorry," I said, trying to catch my breath. "I was upstairs."

I glanced down at the one-hundred-ten-pound brown ball of fuzz at the end of the leash in Jack's hand, surprised he'd brought him.

Like they were old friends, Rynlee lunged forward, throwing her arms around his neck and squealing.

"You brought Merlin?"

"I hope that's okay," he said, shifting in place awkwardly.

"I just thought...we're meeting each other's families, right? Merlin's like my kid."

"No, of course it's okay," I said, stepping back so they could enter. I reached down and patted the dog's head to show I was sincere. "This is perfect."

"Are you sure? You look a little upset. I know you two didn't get off on the best foot, but he's here to make amends, isn't that right?" He rubbed the dog's ears while looking at me hopefully, and I could see how important this was to him.

"I'm positive," I said, putting on a fake smile I hoped would carry up to my eyes as I thought about the house I'd just scrubbed top to bottom, soon to be covered with dog hair. "Look how happy Rynlee is. This made her night." I glanced down at my daughter, who did indeed look over-joyed by her new companion. Finally, Jack stepped into the house and unhooked the leash from the dog's collar.

"Down, Merlin," he said, snapping his fingers and pointing to the ground. To my surprise, the dog's knees almost immediately gave way and he slid to the floor. "He's well behaved most days. I still don't know what got into him the day we met."

"No harm done." I waved my hand casually. "He's forgiven." I smiled at the droopy-faced lab. "Now, let's get dinner started."

The afternoon started out awkward, all of us bouncing around each other carefully, trying not to get in anyone's way, but by the time the spaghetti had been made, the salad tossed, and the pie baked, we'd begun to find our rhythm.

I sat at the head of the table with Rynlee to my left and Jack to my right as he poured our drinks.

"Why are we eating in here?" she asked suspiciously, picking at her food.

"Well, because we have a guest," I said, clearing my throat. "We don't eat in here when Meredith comes over."

My four-year-old never ceased to amaze me with her quick wit and argumentative nature. "Well, Meredith is family. Jack is our guest."

He sat down in the chair and leaned forward, looking directly at Rynlee. "Where do you like to eat?"

She smiled, twirling her fork in her food casually. "In the living room so I can watch *Frozen*."

He chuckled, glancing sideways at me. "Well, it's up to your mom, but I'm fine with that if she is."

I leaned back in my chair with a playful groan. "That's how it's going to be, huh? You two are already pitted against me?"

He stood up, taking my laughter as a sign and lifting his plate. "Hey," he kissed the top of my head as I moved to stand too, "against anyone else in the world, I've got your back. But you against her, I think I have to be on the princess' side."

She giggled, but looked at me for confirmation. "We can go?"

"Mhm." I lifted my plate and hers, carrying them across the room and toward the den. "Whatever you two want."

As we made our way toward the coffee table that Ryn and I used for a dining room table more often than not, Jack scurried past me. He stopped just long enough to whisper "I think I'm nailing it" in my ear before setting his plate next to Rynlee's. "Now, you're going to have to tell me all about *Frozen*," he said. "I've never seen it."

Her eyes grew wide with surprise. "You've never seen *Frozen*?"

He shook his head. "Nope." When she looked away, he

winked at me. "But I'll watch it as much as I need to in order to get caught up."

"You'll regret those words someday," I said smugly, sitting down next to him and taking a bite.

He shook his head, chewing a bite of his own before saying, his voice so low I almost hadn't heard it, "As long as there *is* a someday with you two, there'll be no regrets."

CHAPTER SIX

LOREN

Three Months Later

"Are you ready?" I asked, walking down the stairs with caution. I could smell the cake they'd baked, hear Rynlee's laugh from the kitchen. I'd been confined to my room for the last several hours while Jack and Rynlee threw together the last remaining pieces of my birthday party.

It was sweet how close they'd grown in our time together, even sweeter how much of an effort Jack put into building a relationship with her. My heart was full for the first time in so long, and I had that wonderful man to thank for all of it.

"Ready yet?" I called again, nearing the kitchen. The light flicked off.

"Here she comes," Jack whispered. Then added in a normal voice, "Come on in."

Before I'd even entered the room, Rynlee screamed, "Happy birthday, Momma!" The kitchen was dark, except for the glow of candles—twenty-seven and counting—on the cake's pink icing. Jack held Rynlee up to the table, both with wide grins.

"Happy birthday, Momma," he repeated.

"Oh my gosh, that's what you two were doing down here?" I feigned surprise, my hands to my cheeks. I hugged my daughter, kissing the top of her head before kissing Jack's lips. "This looks delicious."

"It is," Rynlee said, and for the first time, I noticed the chocolate around her lips.

"Mhm, mind if I try?" I asked, running a finger along the edge to scoop up some icing. "You're right, this *is* delicious."

"Jack added strawberries," she said with a giggle. "Your favorite."

"He did, did he?" I raised a brow at him. "Those *are* my favorite."

"Are you surprised?" he asked.

"I am," I said. "Did you cook, too?"

He nodded, pointing toward the pan on the stove. "Cheddar and broccoli soup and loaded baked potatoes."

My stomach grumbled at the thought, my mouth instantly watering. "You two have been busy."

"Are you hungry?" Rynlee asked.

"Starving," I admitted. "Do you have a movie picked out?"

"We're going to eat in here," Jack said. When I looked at him with what must've been a confused expression, he elaborated, "Rynlee's choice."

"You're our guest tonight, Momma." She took my hand, pulling me to the table. "Sit down."

"Your wish is my command," I joked, sitting in the chair she'd led me to.

"And we have a present for you, too," she said. "But you have to close your eyes."

I glanced at Jack, who nodded. "Do as you're told."

"Oh, fine." I closed my eyes, pretending to pout, and held out my hands. Waiting.

Waiting.

Waiting.

The room around me was filled with sudden tension as I listened closely, trying to decide where they'd kept the present hidden. I felt the weight of a small item fill my palm, and I moved my fingers across its velvet sides. The possibility of what I knew it had to be filled my head, but I cast it aside. There was no way. My heart thudded faster in my chest, a mixture of happiness and worry filling me. Was I moving too fast? I hadn't pushed this time. It was all Jack. He'd done the pursuing.

"Open," Jack's whispered command came, and I opened my eyes, staring down at the black velvet box in my hand. *Happiness.* It was the only thing I felt as I looked at the box, knowing what was coming. The worry melted away as quickly as it had come.

"What?" My hands began to shake as I stared at him, down on one knee in front of me, his eyes glistening with tears.

"Open it, Mommy!" Rynlee shouted from just behind him. "See what we got you."

I lifted the lid, staring down at the diamond ring with a lump in my throat as he took my hand. "I love you, Loren. I love you and Rynlee so much. I love our life together—our family. I know it's fast. I know you probably think it's *too* fast, but when you know, you know, and...well, I know." He rubbed his lips together, clearing his throat and tucking a piece of hair behind my ears. "I know that I want to marry you. I know that I want to become your husband. I know that I want to build a life with you, raise a child—maybe children—with you. I know that I want to wake up every morning to hear you snoring next to me or watch the way you cry when someone on *The Voice* gets a four-chair turn. I'm so in love with you. That's all I need to know, and I know that more than I've ever known anything else in my life, so why wait?" He pulled the ring from the box and held it out to me. "Loren Mae Heinz, will you marry me?"

I looked to Rynlee, who was standing behind him with clasped hands and an anxious grin. She nodded, cupping her hands around her mouth in a whisper to me. "Say yes!"

A laugh tore through my tears and I pulled him toward me, unable to form words. My cheek rubbed his, as I nodded my answer, my face buried in his neck.

"Yes?" he asked, pulling me away, his hands cupping my arms.

"Yes," I said. "Of course I'll marry you." He slid the ring on my finger, pressing his lips to mine, and I was sure my heart was going to explode with joy and happiness. Everything I'd always wanted was right in front of me. I'd finally have the family, the love, and the fairytale I'd always dreamed of. I'd been right to say goodbye to Travis. Everything I had with Jack was so much better.

"God, I love you," he said, reaching back to pull Rynlee into our embrace. My heart swelled even more as she hugged him back. "Both of you."

"Did we surprise you?" she asked, her eyes wide.

"You sure did!" I said, wiping away my tears so I could admire the ring. "You two've made me so happy." I kissed her head and then his cheek. "Thank you."

She climbed from my lap and turned on the light. "You're welcome, Mommy. Now, let's eat."

Jack smiled at me, looking down at the ring. "Do you like it?"

"I love it," I said, staring at the intricate vintage detailing. "I love *you*."

He tapped the ring, grabbing the stack of plates from the table. "Well, it's a good thing, 'cause you're stuck with us both."

CHAPTER SEVEN

LOREN

Six Months Later

J ust six months later, we were wed. We'd chosen to have an intimate ceremony at my home, with a larger reception at Jack's bar. Meredith and I had worked tirelessly, hanging flowers from the large, wooden rafters in the rustic, airy room. We'd opened the oversized shutters to bring in daylight, giving the building an entirely different feel. I thought that it would matter—how the room looked or if my hair stayed in place that day. I fussed over the maid of honor dress Meredith would wear and the flower girl dress for Rynlee. I ordered three different best man collars for Merlin to try. I thought it all mattered, but in the end, when I saw him waiting at the bottom of the stairs for me, everything else faded away. What mattered was us. Him. Me. Ryn. All of us together. What mattered was that I loved him and he was mine.

"You look beautiful, my love," Meredith said, squeezing

me into one of her famous, long-lasting hugs once we'd arrived at the reception. She looked over my shoulder to where Jack stood, talking to a group of guests. "You got a good one with him."

I glanced at him, my heart warming. "I think so, too."

"So, what are you going to bring me back from Mexico?" she asked, one brow raised as she elbowed me in the side playfully.

"I'm sure I'll find something. Hey, are you positive you'll be okay to keep Rynlee for that long?"

"It's just a week, Lor, we'll be fine. You two deserve a little alone time. Besides, it's been what...almost twenty years since I've had a kid Ryn's age in my house? I could use a refresher course in case you two get busy making more babies for Auntie Mer to babysit."

I touched my belly instinctively, scowling playfully. "Well, I don't think that's in the plans right away. And my child is not a crash course."

"I'm only joking. Lighten up. Everything will be just fine. You two can go and enjoy yourselves, and we'll be right here when you get back." She looked over my head, taking a step back. When I spun around, my new husband was staring back at me.

"Sorry to interrupt. There's someone I want you to meet," he said, a giant grin on his freshly shaven face.

I looked behind him, wondering what he meant. "Who?"

"My mother," he said, taking my hand.

"I thought your mother wasn't coming?" I asked, suddenly self-conscious, though I doubted there would ever be a day when I was more presentable than my wedding day.

"She surprised us," he said. "Excuse us, Meredith." He

pulled my hand, leading me out of the main room and down a hall. "She won't be staying long—she has to get back home to Dad—but she didn't want to miss it."

"That's wonderful, Jack," I told him, squeezing his hand. His father had fallen ill several years before, but in the last year, his health had taken a turn for the absolute worst. From what he'd told me, each day left with him was a miracle. So, when his parents weren't able to make it to the wedding, of course I'd understood. "I wish we'd known. We could've postponed the ceremony for a few hours so she could've been a part of it."

"Well, I only made the decision on a whim," a voice called from just ahead of me. We stopped short as a woman with icy, white hair and startling dark eyes stepped out of a room to my left. She wore a long, silvery-white gown, her makeup professionally done so her wrinkles seemed practically non-existent and her features were shown off with precision. In short, she was breathtaking, though I was immediately put off by something about her. I couldn't place my finger on it.

"Mom, this is Loren, my wife," Jack said, holding out a hand to gesture toward me. "Loren, this is my mother."

JACK LED us into the stockroom, surprising us all that he could find somewhere quiet.

"It's...it's so great to meet you, Mrs. Wells," I said, studying her face and trying to decide if she was happy with her son's choice in a wife.

"Oh, none of that Mrs. Wells nonsense. Call me Coralee," she said, her voice droll but happy, it seemed. "It's so nice to officially meet you, Loren. Jack talks about you all the time, but with Malcolm so sick, it's been hard to get away. You understand."

"Of course." And suddenly I felt guilty that we hadn't visited them. Why hadn't Jack ever asked me to go to their home and meet them? Herrinville was just a few hours' drive from us. "I'm sorry we haven't met also, but I'm so happy you could make it today. I know it means the world to Jack."

"I couldn't bring myself to miss it," she said. "I only wish I could stay longer." She sighed, heaving her chest. "But, let's not dwell on that. I want to know all about you." Her eyes grew wide. "And your daughter! Oh, where is she? Jack, remind me, she's...four?"

"Five," I corrected. "She just turned five last month. We had a small party, but Jack said you weren't up to traveling." I looked up to him with a question in my expression.

Coralee spoke up suddenly. "That's right. He did ask me. I'd forgotten. Well, happy late birthday to her. So, where'd you say she is?"

"She's...around here somewhere. Probably with Merlin."

"Well, I'm just dying to meet her," she said with a loud laugh. "And see your lovely home. Jack mentioned you'll all be living in your home, right?" She gave me a side-eye and pointed up toward the ceiling. "I've been trying to get him out of this studio bachelor pad for years."

"Yes, we'll be moving into Loren's house," he said with a groan, offering his mother a side hug. "Now, let's go find Rynlee and introduce you two. I'll get you a glass of punch."

"We're perfectly fine here, Jack. I want to get to know the woman who's going to make an honest man out of you, after all." She winked at me, and I flushed red and looked down. I couldn't read her, and that was entirely frustrating to me. "Sit down, son, take a breath." She pointed to a chair next to me and, like a dog, Jack sat.

Her smile was that of a cat, her wise eyes turned into sharp points. "Now, then, where were we..."

CHAPTER EIGHT

LOREN

At Coralee's insistence she'd clean up the reception, Jack and I headed home early. I was tired and exhausted and ready to be with my husband—in every way possible.

We'd already agreed Rynlee would stay with Sarah that night to give Meredith a break before she was on babysitting duty for the whole week, so we'd have the house completely to ourselves—a luxury we hadn't had before.

We stopped on the front porch and Jack placed his arms under me, scooping me up like a baby doll and carrying me over the threshold of our home as I laughed. It was a silly tradition, but one that mattered to me, and I appreciated that it mattered to Jack as well. I rested my head on his shoulder, breathing in his scent—woodsy shampoo and rain water scented soap. When he stood me up in front of him, the smile faded from my lips, nothing funny about the look in his eyes. Passion. Desire.

I lifted my arms to wrap them around his neck, my fingers tracing lines across his skin. He lowered his mouth to mine slowly, his lips parting. I sucked in a deep breath as our mouths connected, losing myself in my husband. He moved his hands to my back, wrapping his arms around me tight.

His fingers fumbled with the buttons, there were twenty-eight to be exact. He'd never get them from this direction. I pulled my lips from his, as much as it pained me to do so, kissing his neck and chest as I parted his shirt. He removed his jacket, his eyes locked with mine with a fiery passion that made my knees weak. I'd never been wanted like Jack wanted me, never wanted a man as much as I wanted him.

My body pulsed with desire, my fingers on fire as I turned away from him, clutching my neck and looking at him over my shoulder. "Undress me, Jack," I whispered, my voice more shaky and less seductive than I'd hoped.

He didn't need to be told twice. His fingers moved over each button with care, his lips connecting with my skin, each button an inch he could move further down. His breath was hot against me, my hair standing on end as I waited for the next button, the next kiss.

When the final button was undone, he let the dress fall to the floor. I stepped out of it, turning to face him with just my panties between us.

He looked me over, his eyes darkening as he moved toward me again, hands outstretched. He cupped my breasts, moving his lips from one to the other, before lifting me up. "I don't know if I can wait to get you upstairs," he whispered, nipping at my ear.

I moaned. "I don't know if I want you to." I pulled his shirt from his shoulders, rubbing my hands over his burning skin. He set me down as he unhooked his belt, our eye contact never breaking. As he kicked off his shoes and removed his belt, I looked down. He was all mine. I didn't have to feel shame for looking him over ever again. I stepped forward, taking him in my hands. He pulsed under my palm, his head rolling back.

Buzzzz. Buzzzz. Buzzzz. Buzzzzz.

His phone vibrated from his pile of clothes on the floor, and I tried to push the sound from my mind as I pulled his face down to meet mine for a kiss. He was tense against my touch, obviously distracted. I released him. "Do you need to check that?" I asked. Of course he was going to say n—

"Just a sec. I'm sorry." He darted away from me as if I had a disease, grabbing his phone from his pants on the floor. He turned it over in his hands and groaned. "I'm so sorry."

"Who is it?"

"It's Mom," he said. "I have to take it."

"Can't it wait?" I gestured toward my naked, waiting body, then felt instantly guilty for doing so. What if something were wrong?

He winced. "I'm sorry. It'll just be a second." He put the phone to his ear without any further discussion, his excitement for me visibly shrinking as he walked from the room. "Mom? Everything okay?" I listened carefully to his conversation, feeling cast aside.

"No, everything's fine here," he said, then laughed. "Oh, thank you." Pause. "Yeah, everything was beautiful. Loren and her cousin worked really hard to make sure it turned out well." Pause. "Okay." Pause. "Yeah, we really appreciate it." Pause. "We're excited, too." Pause. "Okay, well, be careful." Pause. "Yep. I love you, too. Tell Dad hello for me." He walked back into the room, where I stood, still naked, yet a bit more angry. "I love you, too. Talk to you tomorrow. Good night."

He hung up, staring at me. "I'm really sorry."

"Everything was okay, then?"

"Yeah, she was just telling us she'd gotten everything cleaned up and was heading home. She said to tell you everything looked beautiful."

I forced a smile.

"I know you're probably mad," he said finally, moving toward me. "But...I love you." He cupped my breast again, rolling his thumb over my nipple. "And I promise..." He moved his mouth down. "To make it..." His lips traveled further down, the anger in my belly quickly fading away to make room for desire. "Up to you."

CHAPTER NINE

LOREN

J ack was on the phone just outside our bedroom. His voice roused me from sleep, though I tried to fight it. I rolled over, lifting the pillow from my head in defeat and grabbing the glass of water from my nightstand. I'd always been a heavy sleeper, and when I wake, my mouth is like the Sahara.

I sucked the water down quickly, trying to decide between my unquenchable thirst and my desire to hear what my new husband was doing, who he was talking to.

I set the glass back on the table when it was empty, quieting my breathing so I could listen. I couldn't make out the sounds. His voice was there, and the conversation was definitely one-sided, but I couldn't make out a single word.

I sank back onto my pillow, arms over my head as I waited for him to return for me. When the door finally opened, it wasn't soon enough. He looked surprised to see me awake.

"Good morning, beautiful." He glanced at his phone. "I'm sorry, did I wake you?"

"I just missed you," I said, patting the bed where his body should've been. He pounced down next to me, kissing my fingers, then my arm, and working his way up to my cheek.

"Not as much as I missed you," he whispered in my ear before placing a kiss there as well.

"Who were you talking to?" I asked, trying to sound nonchalant.

He let a heavy sigh through his nose. "My mom."

I chewed my lip, the anger from the night before hitting me once again. "Everything okay?"

His fingers went to the bridge of his nose in frustration. "No. It's my dad. Mom doesn't think he's going to make it much longer. Like...seriously this time. When she got back home, the nurse said she doesn't know if he'll make it another night. He's on more morphine than ever before, and she said he's not making any eye contact with her, he won't squeeze her hand. I think this is it." I could tell he was trying not to break in front of me, and it was killing me not to be able to say whatever it was he needed to hear.

"Should we go out there?" I asked, furrowing my brow.

"What?" He seemed to consider it, but quickly shook his head. "No, of course not. We're supposed to be leaving for Mexico tonight. They won't hold the ship for us." His finger grazed my forehead as he moved hair from my eyes. "It'll be okay. We've known this was coming for years now. Every moment I've had with him since he was diagnosed four years ago has been on borrowed time. I just have to be grateful for that."

"He's your dad, Jack. We can go on our honeymoon anytime. This is important."

He finally met my eyes, and I could see that I'd been right, that was what he needed me to say. "But the cruise is already paid for. We can't just be out that money."

"That's why we bought the insurance," I said, running my palm across his arm. "It's going to be okay, I promise."

"Are you sure? I'm so sorry."

"I'm positive. This is more important. Besides, I'd like to meet him. And your mother probably needs us right now. I can't imagine going through that alone can be good for her."

He strained to lean forward and kiss my lips. "How did I get so lucky?"

I smiled at him. "I ask myself that every day."

LATER THAT DAY, we arrived in Herrinville. Jack's parents' house, which he'd described as plain and traditional compared to my Victorian mansion, was anything but plain. The two-story Tudor sat back away from the road with a long, paved path leading up to its front door. Jack and I made our way up the path. To my surprise, Jack knocked rather than just walking in as I had always done with my parents' home.

He stared up at the window above the door, waiting patiently for us to be allowed inside. The air was cool around us, the ground wet from the recent rain. It was a gloomy day, and the black of the house only added to that. Next time we came to visit, I was going to ask Jack if it would be okay for us to bring some flowers to brighten up the drab home. Though I'd use different words, of course.

Finally, we heard noise from inside the house. When the door opened, Coralee's head popped out. "Oh, good, it's you.

Come in, come in." She waved her hand hurriedly, as if we were taking too long.

Stepping through the door was like stepping into an oven. The house was easily ninety degrees, a staggering comparison to the fifty-degree day outside. I pulled my jacket off in a hurry, already feeling sweat beading around my hairline and the back of my neck.

"Is your thermostat broken?" Jack asked, removing his jacket as well.

"No, why?" Coralee asked, looking confused. She was dressed in a white, cashmere sweater and gray slacks. Her hair looked as though she'd spent hours on it and, try as I might, I couldn't find one drop of sweat on her. Was she actually comfortable in this temperature? "Are you both hot? I've been keeping it warmer in here because your father gets so cold." She placed a finger to her lips. "I could probably find some extra blankets for him if you'd like me to lower the temperature…"

"Don't be silly," I said, shaking my head. "No. We'll be fine. I'm already feeling better." It was a lie. I felt like I was melting, but that wasn't my place to say.

Taking me at my word, Coralee walked past me and headed up a staircase and down a hallway to our left. "Jack, would you mind having her wait out here? The room your father's in gets a little crowded with so many of us in there."

Jack looked at me. "I think we can fit all of us," he said.

I placed my hand on his arm to keep him from arguing. "It's okay. I'll be right here." I pointed to a bench in their hallway. "Whenever you need me."

He didn't look comfortable with the idea, but Coralee had already gone into the room at the end of the hall. Eventually, he kissed my head. "I won't be in there long," he promised, and with that, he was gone.

The hallway was dark, and I couldn't get a good idea of where anything was, so like I had said, I sat down on the bench in the hallway and pulled out my phone, opening my Kindle app.

It was hard to focus on the story, hard to lose myself within its pages while there were hushed voices and secrets being told just a few rooms away. I wanted to know what was going on. Maybe that was selfish, but I'd given up my honeymoon to be there and I'd left my daughter with a sitter. I'd made sacrifices to be there with my husband, and I was being left out like I was a stranger, rather than family.

So, thirty-two minutes later, when Jack finally emerged from the room, I tried to put on a smile and pretend I wasn't incredibly frustrated. I stood as he approached.

"How is he?" I asked.

"Not good," he admitted, his eyes watery. "I think she's right. It seems like this could be the end." He took my hand and kissed my knuckles, and my anger faded away. "Would you like to meet him?"

I nodded, my palms sweating as he led me into the room. I tried to conceal my gasp when I saw him. Rather, what was left of him. I couldn't believe he was still alive.

Jack's father, Malcolm, was very frail for a man carrying such a strong name. He was shorter than I'd expected, his thin legs like little rods under the white sheet. His skin was practically translucent, and I could see the veins running through each part of him. There were lesions and red patches across his face, hands, and arms, and warts growing around his eyebrows. It took a strength I didn't know I possessed to keep looking at him when all I wanted to do was look away.

Coralee had disappeared, I assumed through the door across from his bed, so it was just Jack and me alone in the room.

"Dad," Jack said softly, "there's someone I want you to meet." He sat down in the chair next to the bed, pulling me onto his lap. His free hand left my lap and reached for his father's fingers. He rubbed a thumb over his knuckles, his voice cracking as he spoke. "This is Loren, my wife."

His father gave no response, except to keep his chest moving up and down with each breath. Jack moved his hand back from his father's and took mine once more. "I hate seeing him like this," he said. "I used to think he was unbreakable."

I leaned my head toward his, wrapping my arms around his neck to allow him to cry if that was what he needed. He leaned into me, and I felt his emotional weight being transferred.

I looked up, pulling away from him slightly when Coralee entered the room again, carrying a tray of medicine.

She set it on the nightstand next to the bed, offering a look of sympathy to her son. She pulled a vial of medicine from the top drawer of the nightstand.

"Don't you have someone who does that for him?" I asked, the question leaving my mouth before I'd planned for it to. "Like, a nurse?"

She pursed her lips. "We've hired nurses before for his daily care, but they don't take care of him like I do. In the end, this was just easier." She lifted a syringe to the bottle, measuring out a dose, and squeezed it into his IV.

He twitched, but only slightly, his breathing becoming less labored and Jack shuddered underneath my arm.

"I can't believe how bad he's gotten," he said. "I should've come sooner. I should've been here more."

Coralee set the medicine down, hurrying over to sit on the edge of the bed in front of us. She lifted her son's chin so he would be forced to look at her. "You can't blame yourself, Jack. Your father didn't want you here, wasting your life away waiting for him to either get better—which he won't—or die—which he *will* regardless of whether you're here or not. Your father knows you love him, son. And he loves you. He loves you enough that he wants better for you...he wants you to have your own life," she smiled at me, "your own love."

Jack nodded. "I just hate this."

She patted his shoulder. "I know, son. It'll be over soon enough."

No one else saw it and, to this day, I'm not entirely sure I did either, but in that moment, as she spoke the words, I could've sworn I saw Malcolm glance her way for just a second. In his eyes, I could see only fear.

CHAPTER TEN

LOREN

It took two more weeks for Malcolm to finally pass away, but when he did, it shattered everything I thought I knew about my family.

Jack, my always calm and peaceful husband, became a mess of grief and anger. At the funeral, it seemed all he and Coralee could do to hold it together. Once it was over and we were back at the house, surrounded by the memories of what once had been, the two grew withdrawn and bitter.

The next day, when it was time for us to return home, Jack wasn't up to it. I knew it from the worried look in his eye. He needed more time to process, but I couldn't leave Rynlee home with her sitter any longer, and I couldn't get ahold of Meredith. There was no telling what was happening with the store, and I was beginning to get worried. We had to go. The choice was nonexistent.

When I was able to approach him in the hall, for the first time without Coralee's presence, I asked the question I prayed he'd say no to. "Do you need me to leave you here?"

He was silent for a moment, moving a hand to my shoulder. "I don't want to be without you."

It wasn't an answer. "I know, but I can't leave Rynlee with Sarah much longer. She's already done us a huge favor by keeping her this long."

He hung his head down, resting it on my shoulder, and I heard his answer in my ear. "I just need more time. I can't leave her alone."

"I know," I said, batting back tears of my own. We'd been married less than a month, but already I was so attached to him. Rynlee was so attached to him. The thought of going home to a house without him, parenting alone again, when I'd had such a clear vision of what my life would be after the wedding, after I'd let him into my home, life, and family for good—knowing none of those things were going to happen as I'd planned, was enough to destroy me. I was a planner. I liked neatness and order, but there was nothing I could do to clean up this mess. At least not yet. Jack had to stay and I had to return. As much as it hurt, it had to be done. "You stay for a while, take care of things here, and I'll go home and do the same there."

He lifted his head to look at me. "Are you sure?"

"Mhm," I told him, hoping he wouldn't notice my tears.

"You're crying." He brushed a tear from my cheek with his thumb. "I'll come home."

"No, no," I argued, though that was desperately what I wanted. "I'll be okay, I swear. I'm sad to leave you; I wish it could be different."

"Me too," he said. "Are you sure about this?"

Before I could answer, Coralee's footsteps could be heard coming from her bedroom. I kissed his lips in a hurry. "It'll be fine," I promised.

Oh, how wrong I was.

"Ryn?" I called through the quiet house. I heard her footsteps rushing toward me, like music to my ears.

She appeared from the kitchen, fresh jam on her cheeks as she lunged into my arms. "Mommy!" I squeezed her body into mine, so thankful to see her.

"I missed you, baby," I told her, brushing her hair from her eyes so I could plant a kiss on her temple. Sarah was just a few steps behind her, both hands resting on her swollen belly.

"You're home early. I thought you wouldn't be in until tonight," she said, glancing over my shoulder. "Where's Jack?"

I stood, giving Sarah a hug. "He decided to stay for a while, until things...settle down." I glanced down at Rynlee. "How's she been?"

"An angel," Sarah said, blowing a piece of hair from her eyes. "She missed you both, though. How were things...there?"

"Tense," I said. "But that was expected. I think maybe it's a relief that he's gone and they feel guilty about that in some ways, you know? Jack, at least. I can't tell with Coralee."

She nodded. "That's understandable. Loss, even when it's expected, rocks your center of gravity for a while."

"You're right, I just hate it for them both." I scooped up my daughter from the floor and balanced her on my hip. "What do I owe you?"

Sarah shook her head, waving her hand. "No, you don't owe me for this. It was no trouble, and I could use the practice for when this little one comes along."

"No, I meant to pay you. I'd never expect you to keep her for this long for free."

She rubbed her swollen belly again. "Just promise you'll keep him at some point and give Dalton and me a fair chance at a date night, and we'll call it even." She laughed. "Seriously, he's on nights this week, so I had nothing else to do. This was a nice change for me."

I hugged her again. "You're a lifesaver. I can't thank you enough for doing it on such short notice again. Speaking of, have you heard from Meredith yet?"

She frowned. "No, I figured you knew what was going on by now. My mom said the shop's been closed."

I groaned and rolled my eyes, frustration filling me. It was one thing to disappear on a whim and leave me without a sitter, Rynlee wasn't her problem. But to leave the shop without anyone working was a whole other issue. "Okay, I'll figure it out." I mentally made a note to check in with the latest guy she'd been seeing—Beau? Was that his name? Bill? —if I didn't hear back from her soon. I'd have to check her Facebook to contact him. If she wasn't with him, I'd look up the touring schedule of a few of her favorite bands. She'd followed an entire tour from state to state a few years back, but that was only once. I wanted to say I was surprised by her disappearance when she was supposed to be keeping Rynlee, but I couldn't put anything past her, as much as I loved her. She was flighty through and through. Honestly, though, I felt a bit betrayed by this, especially when it concerned the business. I'd honestly believed those days were behind us. It had been more than a year since she'd done anything this reckless, especially without giving me a warning. I thought the shop was grounding her a bit. "Thanks again," I said, noticing Sarah was still standing there, waiting for me to say something else. "I've got it from here."

She smiled, bending down slowly to give Rynlee a hug. "See you later, kiddo," she said, ruffling her hair. With that, she waddled past me, patting my shoulder as she went, and headed out the door.

I pulled my phone from my pocket, sending Meredith a quick text.

Where have you been? Need to hear from you ASAP! Xx

I shoved the phone back in my purse and leaned down to scoop Rynlee up. "Did you miss me?" I asked.

"Only a little," she teased, her fingers held up to show a tiny amount.

"Only a little, huh?" I asked, tickling her belly until she squealed in defeat.

"I was only kidding," she informed me, wrapping her tiny arms around my neck. "I always miss you, Mommy. Where's Jack?"

"He had to stay with his mommy for a little while, sweetheart."

"But why?"

"Because she was sad and he needed to be there for her." I carried her into the kitchen and placed her on the counter, sending up a silent thank you to Sarah as I stared into my empty sink. The woman truly was a godsend. I'd have to remember to send her a thank you basket from the store.

Speaking of, I desperately needed to get down there and see what was going on there.

"Hey, do you want to go on a car ride with Mommy?" I asked, scooping her back up and heading for the door.

"Sure," she said. "Why was his mommy sad?"

"Because she lost someone very important to her, baby."

"Who?"

I set her down, pulling a jacket on over her shoulders and pulling my keys from my pocket. "Her husband. Jack's father."

Her eyes widened. "Oh, no. Poor Jack."

"Yes," I agreed sadly. "Poor Jack, but honey, he'll be okay."

"Will he come back and stay with us again?"

I nodded, our steps down the stairs of our porch bouncing us along the way. "Of course he will, Ryn. He lives here now. With us. He'd never want to be anywhere else."

"Merlin misses him," she said, slumping her head down on my shoulder, and I couldn't help but wonder if Merlin was the only one who missed him. Based on the sad eyes that met mine as I buckled her in and the fact that they'd grown so close in such a short time, I'd say the answer to that was no.

"I know, sweetheart. We all miss him." I smoothed her hair back from her face and kissed her head. "He'll be home soon."

HE WASN'T, though—home soon. Another week passed slowly, each text message lifting me with hope just to crash me back down to the ground when he revealed he still wasn't coming home.

Rynlee sat at the breakfast table that morning, picking aimlessly at her eggs. She missed him, we all did, but he'd showed no signs of returning to us. In fact, in the few phone calls we'd had, he seemed more distant than ever. Had I given our marriage its death sentence by letting him stay away for so long? By forgoing our honeymoon? It had seemed like the right thing to do at the time, but now, I wasn't so sure.

When the phone chimed that morning, I bounded up, flipping it over and staring at the screen.

It was Meredith again. Though she wasn't who I was hoping to hear from, her name on my screen brought instant relief. My last text had gotten only a one sentence reply: **Be in touch soon. Xx**

This message explained a bit further: **Sorry I've been MIA. Met a guy at the wedding...can't wait to tell you about him. So cute! Be home when I can.**

I rolled my eyes at the response, feeling frustrated at how cavalier she sounded: **What about the store? Jack's father passed away and we really needed you—**

I stopped, backing out of the message. I couldn't do that. My problems weren't hers. Meredith's daughter was grown. She deserved to find happiness, and I couldn't fault her for that.

I'll ask Becky to take on some extra shifts at the store, I said instead. **Hope you're having fun. Be safe. We love you. Xx**

With that, I sent the message, appearing casual and breezy, though I felt anything but. I missed my friend. I needed someone to talk to about all that was going on in my life, but how could I expect her to pass up an opportunity to snag what Jack and I had?

As if summoned by the mere thought of him, my phone buzzed again. This time, it was Jack's name on my screen. I nearly dropped the phone trying to answer it so quickly.

"He-hello?" I called into it before the speaker had touched my ear.

"Hey," he said, his voice flooding me with sadness and

hope. I held my breath instinctively as I waited for him to say he was staying another week.

"How are you?"

"I'm okay." His voice was low. Wherever he was, he was trying to keep our conversation quiet. I glanced at the clock, it was half past seven. Maybe Coralee was still asleep and he was trying not to wake her. "I miss you."

"You do?" I asked, raising a brow as I stepped away from the table, making sure to keep an eye on my daughter as she gave pieces of her breakfast to Merlin.

"Of course I do," he said. "I wish I was there right now."

"Me too," I admitted. "Speaking of...when *do* you think you'll be here?" I tried to seem like the question had just popped into my head, rather than let him know the truth—that it was all I could think of.

He sighed. "Hopefully soon. Mom's...I had hoped she'd be handling this better by now, but she's not. They'd been married for more than thirty years, you know? It's not easy to forget that. I'm trying to help her sort through some of his stuff, get things in order, but it's...it's just hard. I'm not sure if I'm helping or making things worse at this point."

"I'm sure you're helping," I assured him. "And I know she appreciates you being there."

"Well, thank you for saying that," he said. "It doesn't always feel like it."

"Is there anything I can do?"

He was silent for a moment. "You've got so much on your plate already. I can't give you anything else."

Which meant he wanted to. "Of course you can. I'm here, what can I do?"

"*If* you have time, seriously don't worry about it if you don't, but *if* you do, I was going to see if you could stop by the bar at some point this week and make sure the vendor dropped everything off yesterday. I got the confirmation, but sometimes things don't match the order and Darryl isn't always the best at checking those things."

I swallowed. "O-okay. That's fine. I have to go into town to give Becky lunch breaks every day, anyway. I'm happy to do that for you."

"Meredith still isn't back?" he asked.

"No, not yet, but I finally heard from her. She's with some guy."

"She just left you to deal with things?" He sounded angry suddenly, but he had no right to be. It wasn't like he wasn't doing the same thing. I pushed the thought from my mind.

"It's fine, I can handle it. I was planning to leave her to deal with things while we were on our honeymoon, anyway."

"Yeah, but apparently she would've bailed on that."

"It's fine, Jack, honestly. I can handle everything."

"I know you can, but you shouldn't have to. Rynlee, the house, your shop, the bar, Merlin, for crying out loud." He sighed. "I've got to come home."

"Really?" I couldn't hide the cheer from my voice as he said it.

"I don't think I have a choice, it's too much on you."

"So, you don't *want* to come home?" Vulnerability seeped out. I couldn't help it, as much as I hated it.

"What—no. Of course I want to come home."

"I can handle it, I really can. If you need to stay, you should stay."

"Do you want me home, Loren?" he asked, his voice lower than before.

I wanted to deny it, to tell him everything was fine, but I couldn't. "You're my husband. I want to be with you."

"I want to be with you, too, honey. I do. I want that more than anything."

"Then, come home," I said, letting the final wall crumble.

"What am I supposed to do about Mom?"

"What are you planning to do? Stay there forever?"

"No! Not forever. Just until she's stable again."

"How long will that take, Jack? At least another week, you've made that clear."

"I don't want to fight with you," he said, and I suddenly felt like the world's biggest asshole.

"I don't want to fight with you either," I said, sighing with a hand over my face. Rynlee was blissfully oblivious to the conversation as she handed Merlin her last piece of egg and held her plate in the air.

"Done!" she announced.

I pushed myself away from the counter, walking over to the table and taking her plate. "Look, what if you brought your mother here for a while? Get her out of the house. It might do her some good."

He made a noise between a scoff and a groan. "I don't know. Are you sure?" Did he sound relieved or fearful? I couldn't tell.

"Why not? We have plenty of room here, and we could all keep her busy, keep her company, until she's feeling better and ready to be on her own. It might be nice."

"I don't think you know what you're signing up for," he said. "My mother can be...*difficult*."

"She's family, Jack. That's what matters. And besides, if she comes, I get you back home where you belong. That's *really* what matters."

He paused. "As much as I want to be home with you, are you absolutely sure about this?"

"I'm positive. It'll give me a chance to get to know her better. And she's the only living grandparent Rynlee will ever know. I'd like for them to bond. Besides, how bad could she be?"

If I'd only known...

CHAPTER ELEVEN

LOREN

"Rynlee, they're here," I called into the living room, watching my daughter jump up and rush toward me with excitement.

"Come on, Merlin," she yelled at the sleeping lab near her feet. He lifted his head slowly, his mouth opening in one, long yawn. The two rushed for the front door, watching the black sedan pull into the driveway.

"Now, remember," I said, repeating the instructions I'd been drilling into her head, "Ms. Coralee is our guest. You're to be on your best behavior, okay? We want to make her feel welcome. That means toys stay in your bedroom and out of the way, and you have to be quiet whenever she's asleep. At dinner, there'll be no fits about what we're having, okay?"

"Yeah, okay," she said, nodding in agreement, though her eyes were affixed on Jack as he hurried around to the passenger side to open his mother's door. I pushed open the front door, stepping out onto the porch with Rynlee in tow. Merlin barrelled past us, obviously setting his sights on his true owner. Jack, spying him, bent down to give his pet a pat on the head.

"I missed you, old man," he said.

As I grew nearer, he stood. "Hey, you."

"Hey, you," I said back. "I've missed—"

"Jack," Coralee's distraught voice shot out of the car, interrupting me. "Can you get my bag, please? It's much too heavy for me."

Jack looked away from me, jumping to his mother's aid at once. He took the large, black bag from her outstretched hand, helping her stand from her seat and shut the door.

"It's nice to see you again, Coralee," I said, patting Rynlee's back. "We're so happy to have you stay with us."

Her smile was distant and cold. She barely offered a glance in Rynlee's direction, though my on-her-best-behavior daughter stood there, smiling politely at the stranger who was invading her home.

"Can you help Jack with the rest of the bags?" Coralee asked, pointing over her shoulder toward the trunk.

"Oh, of course," I said, jumping into action. *Rest?* The bag in Jack's hand was already more than enough for a week's worth of clothes. When I got to the back of the car, Jack had already popped the trunk. To my surprise, there were four more bags waiting for us, all even larger than the one in Jack's hands.

"This is...a lot," I whispered.

He nodded, his mouth forming a grimace. "She wanted to feel at home. I'm sorry."

"That's understandable," I told him, grabbing a bag and hoisting it over my shoulder. Why shouldn't she want to feel at home? It wasn't a vacation. She was supposed to be healing. Surely that would come easier surrounded by the comforts of home. I grabbed one more, sure I was going to have considerable damage to my spine if I managed to make it in the door with them, and Jack grabbed the last two. Together, we made our way up the stairs with Coralee leading the way.

"Ryn, could you get the door for Ms. Coralee?" I asked, forcing out a breath as we seemed to be moving at an even slower pace than before. It would've been rude to dash around our guest in an attempt to set the bags down, but it was all I wanted to do.

"I'm perfectly capable of getting the door for myself," came Coralee's tightlipped response.

"Oh, of course," I said, feeling as though I'd been slapped. Coralee grabbed the door, pulling it open and stepping inside. I stuck my foot out to keep the door from slamming shut in Rynlee's face. She looked up at me with concern. "Go on," I assured her. I'd spent so much time preparing my daughter to be polite to our guest. I hadn't thought to prepare her for if our guest wasn't polite back.

When we entered the living room, I set the bags down as quickly as possible, massaging my arms with a sigh of relief. "Those were heavier than I thought," I said with a laugh.

"Are you okay?" Jack asked, setting his down and moving to stand next to me.

"I'm all right," I said, smiling at him. It was nice to have him home, nice to have his attention on me once again.

"I'd like to go to my room," Coralee announced, looking around the house. "It's upstairs, I presume."

"Yes," I told her. "We've got you set up with your own wing. You'll have a bedroom and a bathroom all to yourself, so you can have some privacy." I smiled. "And you won't be disturbed if things get too loud down here," I cast a playful glance toward my daughter.

Coralee nodded stiffly. "Show me where it is, then."

I moved to pick up her bag, but Jack stopped me. "I'll come back for those."

"Thank you," I said, making my way toward the stairs. When we got to the third floor, I turned down the long hall that would lead to Coralee's space.

"It's dark up here," she said.

I flipped on the hall light. "Sorry. We're used to all the windows letting in some light, but it's a rather gloomy day. This is your room right down here. I pointed to the left. "There's the bathroom directly beside it. There's also a door in the room that'll take you there too, so you don't have to leave your room at night."

"Or anytime, seems to be your hope," she said.

"Mom!" Jack scolded. "That was rude."

My jaw dropped. Her coldness hadn't gone unnoticed, but I was completely blown away by her comment. "I'm sorry, Coralee, if I've done something to upset you. I didn't mean that at all. We're happy to have you with us, anywhere with us, I just wanted you to feel like you'd have your privacy here as well."

She turned the doorknob that led to her bedroom, stepping inside without a word. She stared around the room, taking in her new space while I waited for her to address her actions. Instead, she turned around, looking at Jack. "Leave the bags here, and I'll get unpacked. You two can go."

Two. She was completely ignoring Rynlee.

"Mom, you should apologize to Loren and Rynlee," Jack

said, dropping her bags. "They've done a lot to arrange for you to come. It was Loren's idea. You're being rude."

Coralee looked at me out of the corner of her eye, not even bothering to turn her body to face me. "Thank you, Loren, for putting up with the *inconvenience* of a grieving widow."

"You're not an inconvenience," I tried to tell her, "we're—"

"I'd like to be alone now," she said, her tone sharp as she placed her hand on the door. My daughter gripped my hand tighter, and I felt her fear coursing through me, filling me with anger. How dare she come into my house and act like she was?

Without another word, I turned on my heel and scooped Rynlee up, headed back down the hall and downstairs. Jack's footsteps were close behind. Once we'd arrived on the first floor, he wrapped the two of us in a hug, kissing Rynlee's head. "You'll have to excuse her," he said. "She's been like this since Dad's passing. I'm starting to worry it's..." He looked at Rynlee. "Getting bad."

I nodded. "It's okay. We're just glad to have you home," I told him, resting my head on his shoulder and breathing in his soapy scent. Oh, how I'd missed him.

"I'm glad to be home. You have no idea."

"We have so much to tell you," Rynlee said excitedly, transferring from my arms to Jack's when he held them out.

"You do, do you? Like what?"

She grinned as he carried her into the kitchen. "Well, Merlin's getting really fat since he moved in here," she said with a giggle. "He likes my food."

Jack set her on the counter, listening intently as she told him all about her time since he'd been gone. Occasionally, he'd cast a glance my way, offering a smile or a wink. It was good to have him home—my husband—even if it meant I had to put up with the nagging feeling I'd made a mistake letting my mother-in-law come, too.

CHAPTER TWELVE

LOREN

We didn't see Coralee again until the next day. I'd been worried when she didn't come down for dinner, but Jack insisted we let her be. He said she just needed time to settle in and that she was probably feeling foolish for the way she'd behaved.

I didn't want that. I didn't want her to feel foolish, I just wanted us to all get along. My house had always been a place of comfort for myself and Rynlee, I hated the on-edge feeling I now had within its walls.

When I heard her footsteps descending the stairs, I looked at Jack, trying to convey the worry I felt without saying anything in front of Rynlee.

She moved slowly, keeping us in anticipation longer than I felt necessary, and when she finally entered the room, she didn't speak right away. Instead, she sunk into the chair across from me at the table.

Three seconds passed before she looked up.

"My life is hard right now," she said. It wasn't an apology. She took a breath. "My life is...it's very hard right now. I know you think because I had time to prepare that it shouldn't be so hard, but—"

"We don't think that, Mom," Jack said, pulling her attention to him. "Neither of us."

She looked back at me, waiting for confirmation, and I nodded. "He's right. I lost my parents a few years ago, so I know how bad you must be feeling. I don't know of anything that could've lessened that pain for me, time to prepare included." Was that really what she thought? That I was angry with her for wallowing? "I meant what I said yesterday, Coralee. We are so happy to have you here with us. Rynlee and I would love to get to know you better, and I know Jack will enjoy having you around for a while. If I did something to make you feel like you weren't welcome, I truly apologize."

Coralee sat up straighter, looking pleased with the conversation. "Well, good then. I'm happy we could work that out." With that, she stood and walked out of the room. "Coffee?" I heard her voice ring out from the kitchen.

"Coming," Jack called with laughter in his tone, standing up from the table. He kissed my fingertips, ruffling Rynlee's hair playfully. "I think that's as close to an apology as I've ever heard from her," he whispered, and with that he departed, headed to his mother's rescue.

———

LATER THAT DAY, I knocked on Coralee's door with apprehension. After her coffee, she'd announced she was going to take a bath, and I hadn't seen or heard from her since.

"Coralee?" I called, when she didn't answer after a few knocks. I hoped she wasn't napping. I waited a moment longer, trying to decide whether or not to walk away, when the door finally swung open.

"Is everything okay?" she asked, her voice out of breath. She had a heavy robe wrapped around her body, her hand clutching the slit of it so her chest wouldn't be revealed. She appeared frazzled, and her room smelled strongly of lavender and sage. I paused. Was she just lying around my house...*naked*?

"Yes, of course," I said finally, shoving the thought from my brain. "Sorry, I didn't mean to disturb you. Um, Rynlee and I have to run to town, to my store, to give one of the employees a lunch break. Jack's gone to work, too. I wanted to see if you'd like to join us?" The end of my sentence was an octave higher than the rest as I tried to decide if the question was a mistake. I wanted to make an effort to show her I cared, but I felt like a child speaking to her, waiting to be scolded. What was it about her that made me feel that way?

Her lips upturned slightly, though the smile didn't reach her eyes, and she bowed her head. "Yes, I'd love to. What a great idea. Let me just get changed really quickly. You've caught me in the middle of a nap."

"Okay," I said. "That's fine. We'll be downstairs whenever you're ready." With that, she shut the door and I made my way back down the stairs.

"Rynlee, come on, baby. Come get your jacket," I called, helping my daughter pick up the toys from the floor. When we were done, I put her jacket on and locked Merlin behind the baby gate in the laundry room.

Then, we waited.

And waited.

Half an hour went by as I paced the floor, trying to keep my child occupied while she squirmed and begged to drag her toys back out. As we neared forty-five minutes, I made my way back toward the stairs.

"Coralee? Everything okay?" I called, trying to keep the agitation from my voice.

"Come on, Mommy!" Rynlee whined, hanging on my arms and trying to pull me toward the door.

"Hang on, baby," I told her for the hundredth time. "We're going to leave soon, I promise." I looked back up the stairs. "Coralee?"

When she didn't answer, I scooped up my daughter, carrying her up the stairs and toward my new mother-in-law's room once more. Two flights of stairs later, I knocked carefully. "Coralee? Is everything okay in there?"

"Yes it is. Why do you ask, dear?" came her immediate response through the door.

I shook my head in confusion. "Well, I thought we were getting ready to leave. My employee will be needing her break soon."

"Right, right," she said, and I heard her feet moving across the hardwood floors. Finally, she opened the door, still in her robe. "Sorry, dear, I'm looking for something to wear. It'll just be another minute."

I couldn't believe it. "O-okay," I said, trying to determine what words would sit well with either of us. "Are you sure? I don't mean to rush you, it's just that I'll need to give my employee lunch soon. It's almost one, and she's been there all morning."

She huffed. "Yes, yes, so you've said. Just a minute. I can't very well get dressed with my door standing wide open, now can I?" With that, the door was shut in my face and I glanced down at my daughter.

"She's grumpy, isn't she, Mommy?" she asked, a crooked little grin on her face.

I grimaced and pulled her back from the door, bending down so I could whisper in her ear. "You shouldn't say things like that, okay? Just in case she were to hear you and get her feelings hurt." I rested my forehead on hers to assure her she wasn't in trouble. "But you're right." She nodded, but didn't say another word.

Several minutes later, I heard Coralee making her way down the stairs. When she arrived on the first floor, she stood in front of us, wearing a velvet jacket over black slacks. "Are you ready, then?"

I gave her a stiff nod, hoping my smile looked genuine. "Let's go."

Fifteen minutes later, we were pulling into the store's parking lot. The car ride had been a quiet one. Despite Rynlee's request for music, Coralee had insisted on riding in silence due to what she called a *monstrous* headache.

I removed Rynlee from her car seat and set her on her feet in front of the door, watching her bound into the shop and straight for Becky's arms, while I held the door open for Coralee. She glanced around and, to my surprise, there was a grin on her face.

"Why, this is a cute little shop you have." She looked across the store, her eyes dancing around the room before landing on me. "You own this?"

I nodded. "I do, with my cousin, Meredith."

"And this is Meredith?" she asked, holding her hand out to Becky. Suddenly, she was ever so charming.

"No. This is Becky," I informed her. "Our employee." Then, I addressed Becky, "Becky, this is Coralee. My mother-in-law."

Becky nodded at Coralee. "Nice to meet you."

Coralee released her hand. "You too."

Finally, it was my turn to speak, "I'm sorry we were late. How's everything been here?"

"Fine," she drawled. "We sold out of the tulips and daisies, but Meredith has been ordering extra, so I think we'll be okay when the shipment gets here in the morning. Oh, and we sold two more of Meredith's purses. She'll be pleased."

I looked over to the flower counter, delighted to see she was right. "Well, I guess those few days of being closed didn't hurt us too badly, then, did it?" I moved over to the desserts. "How are we doing on these?"

"We haven't sold too much," she said. "A few cookies here and there, but I don't think we've sold any of the brownies all week. The pies seem to do well, but it's hit or miss."

I nodded. "Okay, well, if nothing else it's all market research, right?"

"Do you want me to keep making them, or...?"

I frowned. "I don't know." It'd been Meredith's idea to start making the desserts, and I hated the thought of nixing her plan without talking to her first. "Let's keep it up another week, especially what you see actually selling, but—*no!*" I screamed, lunging forward as Rynlee's hand reached for a pie sitting near the edge. My sudden outburst seemed to scare her, and she stepped back, her bottom lip quivering as her eyes filled with tears. I lifted her to my chest, pressing her head into my neck as my heart thudded with fear. "What have we said about these?" I asked, the question directed at Becky.

She stared at the pie, trying to understand what had upset me, and I pointed at the peanut symbol on the front.

"I'm sorry, Loren. Oh, God, I'm so sorry. I don't know

how that one got up front. I'm always so careful." She rushed around to the front of the counter and stared at the desserts. "See, they're all in the back except that one. A customer must've moved it to the front."

"It wasn't your fault." I calmed slightly as I looked Rynlee over. "I'm sorry I scared you," I told my daughter. When I looked back at Becky, I said, "I didn't mean to freak out. We should've never tried to make anything peanut butter in the first place. Rynlee's here too much to chance it. I'll make sure Meredith takes it off the list. After this batch, don't make anymore. When you close up tonight, let's throw it out. There have been one too many close calls for me."

Coralee stepped back into my line of vision; she'd been so quiet perusing the store I'd almost forgotten she was there. "For goodness sake, what is going on?" she demanded. "What's the matter?"

"Rynlee is very allergic to peanuts," I explained. "And she almost pulled a pie down. Even a little bit on her skin could send her into anaphylactic shock."

She narrowed her gaze at my daughter. "How terrible."

"Everything's okay," I said, kissing her head. "It was just a little scare." I looked at Becky, who was still staring wide-eyed at the table, her haunted expression showing she felt the weight of what almost happened. "It wasn't your fault," I reiterated. "These things can't always be helped. Let's just set this back here," I placed the peanut butter pie at the back of the counter, " and you can go on ahead to lunch."

She nodded, still looking upset. "I'm really sorry, again. I would've never forgiven myself if—"

"There's nothing to forgive. I should've been keeping a closer eye on things. You've been the only one here when Meredith and I are usually around to help you out." I touched her hand. "I appreciate you stepping up when we've needed you."

With that, the last of her worry seemed to fade and she smiled back, squeezing Rynlee's arm playfully. "I'm always happy to help. I'll be back in half an hour," she said, disappearing out the front door.

When she left, Coralee huffed, staring after her. "Incompetent help never did anyone any good, Loren. You'll do good to recognize that."

"Oh, Becky's not incompetent. It was an honest mistake," I told her. "She's been with us since we opened, and truly, I don't think we'd still be open without her."

Her expression was stiff; I could see she didn't agree. "An honest mistake might be all it takes next time."

Without another word, she went back to evaluating the store, and I moved around behind the counter with Rynlee to begin going over the books. I tried to put what she'd said to the back of my mind, but it'd be a lie to say it ever truly left. What if she was right?

CHAPTER THIRTEEN

LOREN

The rest of the week was surprisingly calm. Despite Coralee's presence in the house, we hardly saw her. When dinner was made, she'd request to eat alone in her room, and with her bathroom and bedroom conjoined, it didn't seem she ever planned to leave.

So, on Sunday when I came into the kitchen to the smell of bacon sizzling on the stove, I was shocked to find her there—spatula in hand.

"C-Coralee?" I asked, wrapping my robe tighter around me.

"I thought you'd gone out." She turned to see me, her eyes wide for a moment before the shock wore off.

"Why would you think that?" I asked, shaking my head.

"The car left this morning," she said simply, turning back to her bacon.

"It did?" I glanced over my shoulder out the window, though I couldn't see the spot where the car should've been from there. "I assumed Jack was down here." I pulled my phone from my robe pocket, but the screen was blank. "He didn't say where he was going?"

"Shouldn't *you* know that? He's your husband."

I tried to ignore the comment, though I couldn't deny the fresh sting I felt on my skin. She was right. I *should* know. It wasn't like him to just disappear. Distracting me from my thought, I heard little footsteps rushing down the hallway. I stepped out of the kitchen so I could see her coming.

"I got it, Ms. Coralee," Rynlee yelled, holding an apron in the air as she rushed toward me. "Good morning, Mommy!"

"Good morning, sweetheart. What have you got there?" I bent down as she neared me, taking the cloth from her hand. "Your apron?" The apron was white with a pink rolling pin on the front and in silver script, it read *Mini Chef.* It had been a gift from Meredith a few Christmases back.

"Mhm, Ms. Coralee was going to let me cook with her, but she said a lady should always have an apron in the kitchen." She cocked her head to the side. "Do you have an apron, Mommy?"

I forced a smile and ruffled her hair. "No, I don't, sweetie. Mommy will have to get one someday."

"You can borrow mine," she informed me, "but not today." With that, she rushed past me and into the kitchen. I followed her, scrolling through my recent calls to find Jack's name.

Just as I found it, I caught a distinct smell wafting through the kitchen. A smell that had never been allowed in my home.

"Peanut butter?" I whispered, glancing around. Then, louder, "Coralee, do you have peanut butter?"

She nodded in the direction of the oven underneath her. "I made cookies," she said. "Rynlee was going to help me cut them once they're done." She grinned at my daughter. "Show her the cookie cutter you've picked out."

"She can't be around peanut butter, Coralee, I've told you that," I said angrily, scooping up my daughter and pulling her away from the stove. "Even just a good enough amount in the air or on her skin could cause a reaction. *She could die!*"

Coralee turned away from her pan completely, staring at me with wide, innocent eyes. "I had no idea, Loren. I'm sorry."

"I told you at the store the other day," I argued. "If you'd let her cut them with you, she would've gone into shock. Do you understand how serious all of this is? How did you even get peanut butter into the house?"

"I went to the store a few nights ago when I couldn't sleep," she said, "and I don't remember you telling me this. If you did—"

"I did." I pointed at the stove. "Turn it off. We have to throw it out. All of it. The peanut butter, too."

"That seems extreme," she began. "I can keep it in my room away from Rynl—"

"*This is my house!*" I screamed at her, my resolve completely lost. "And you will not have anything in it that could endanger my daughter."

I heard the front door slam, and we both turned to look in its direction when I heard Jack's voice.

"What's going on?" he asked, entering with a paper sack in his arms.

"Where were you?" I demanded.

"Mom asked me to go and get some flour and butter. We were out." He pulled a few things from the sack to prove a point. "Why? What happened?"

I glared at Coralee. "*You* asked him to go? And then you

thought I went with him and you made peanut butter cookies for Rynlee?"

"You did what?" Jack asked, the weight of the situation clear in his tone.

"I didn't know the child was allergic," Coralee said. "You're making me out to be a monster here when my only crime is trying to get to know my new grandchild." She reached behind her and flipped off the stove. "I'm sorry if I've upset you or endangered your daughter, but I've only just met the both of you. You can't expect me to know everything about you already. And she's fine—"

"Because I came down here and stopped it before you could feed them to her."

Jack put a hand on my arm to calm me. "She didn't know, Lor. I know it's terrifying, but she didn't."

"She did!" I argued. "I told her. I told her earlier this week."

She shook her head. "I'm an old woman, Loren. My mind isn't as sharp as yours. If you did tell me, I must've forgotten."

"You can't forget this!" I said, pulling Rynlee's head into mine.

"Okay," Jack said, his voice louder than both of ours. "Okay, let's all just calm down. It was a mistake, but we caught it. Mom," he looked at her seriously, "you cannot bring peanut butter into the house. Ever. Rynlee's allergy is serious. Tell me you understand that."

"I do, of course I do. It'll never happen again." She glanced at me, but there was no apology in her eyes. "My mother... had dementia. She died from it when I was young. My memory isn't what it once was, but...I don't think it's that." She shook her head, disagreeing with herself. "No. It's not. It can't be." She looked up at me with wide, fearful eyes. "I think I'll just head up to my room again. This argument has taken so much out of me." She placed the back of her hand on her forehead, feigning exhaustion as she walked from the room without another word. When her footsteps had grown faint enough I was sure she couldn't hear us, I faced my husband.

"Jack," I said, my head shaking. I needed him to believe me. I needed him to see my side.

He pulled Rynlee and me into a hug, rubbing my back. "I'm so sorry," he said, kissing the side of my head. "I'm *so sorry*. I'd never forgive myself if—" He cut the sentence short, unable to say it just as much as I felt unable to think it.

"Why would she do this?" I asked him, pulling away so I could meet his eyes. Before he could answer, I walked from the room and into the dining room, pulling out a coloring book and a few crayons for Rynlee. "Here, baby, you color with this while Mommy cleans up, okay?"

She nodded, her sideways glances toward me showing she was still shaken up by the interaction she'd witnessed, and she began to flip through the book for the perfect page. Once she was distracted, I turned back to my husband, taking his arm and pulling him out of the room. I stood so I could still keep a good eye on Rynlee, but not close enough she could hear our whispers.

"I don't think it could've possibly been on purpose, Loren. She wouldn't have..." He trailed off. "She's not in her right mind right now. And she's getting older, she forgets things. You heard what she said about her mother having dementia. It's something she's always worried about."

"Do you really believe she's sick? You've never mentioned her having issues with memory before."

"She hasn't," he said thoughtfully. "Not that I remember."

"She can't...she can't *forget* something like that, Jack. And she thought I was going to be gone with you—and she didn't mention that you'd gone to do a favor for her in the first place—what if we'd both been gone, Jack? Rynlee's EpiPen is in my purse. We have a spare locked under the sink that Meredith and Sarah know about, but your mother wouldn't have. She would've...she wouldn't have made it. This can't happen again..." I was nearing hysterics, my vision blurring with tears as I realized just how close I'd come to losing everything.

"It won't," he promised. "I won't let it."

"I need to get the peanut butter out of the house," I said, the smell of it making me nauseous with worry.

"No," he said, taking my hand to stop me. "I'll take care of it. You take Rynlee outside to play for a bit, and I'll clean everything and get it outside in the garbage."

"Are you sure?"

"It's the least I can do."

"Your mother needs to wash her hands," I paused, "oh, and the dishes, we need to make sure anything that touched the peanut butter is scrubbed...the bacon will have to be thrown out...and you'll need a shower after it's been cleaned."

He nodded, letting out a slow breath. "I've got this," he said, his eyes meeting mine seriously. "I promise you. I'll get everything taken care of. I won't risk anything hurting her."

I smiled at him, but it wasn't a smile that reached my eyes. My mind was elsewhere, racing through all that had gone wrong and all that still could. I replayed the instructions her doctor had given me after the first time she'd had a reaction. I remembered the way the hives came on fast, how she'd run out of air before we made it to the hospital.

No.

I pushed the thought from my head, walking toward her. "Thank you," I said to him, lifting her up without warning and walking from the house. I needed some air.

———

THAT NIGHT, after Rynlee was put to sleep, I lay in bed, staring at the ceiling. I couldn't make myself sleep. I was too worried. Too frantic. Everything felt dangerous now. What else had Coralee brought into my house? What else had I allowed into my home?

"How are you?" Jack asked, pulling his shirt from his head and slinking across the bed toward me.

I smiled halfheartedly, pinching the excess skin around my pinkie nail. "I'm okay."

He kissed my hands. "I promise you I scrubbed every inch of this house that peanut butter could've gotten anywhere near. The dishes are all bleached and the cookies are double bagged and already in the garbage can outside."

"I know," I told him for the fifth time. I knew he'd done all he could, but it did nothing to ease my mind. "And you talked to your mom, right? You made her understand how serious it is?"

"I did," he said, his lips grazing my jawline as his hand slid across my belly, his fingers creeping up under my T-shirt. He pulled away, pausing his movements. "I told her, and I made her throw out the peanut butter. She promised she wouldn't ever bring it back into the house, and she's...she's so sorry, Loren. She feels terrible, really."

"She doesn't seem to."

"She's embarrassed. She doesn't like to admit she forgets

things anyway, but to admit she forgot something like this…
to have endangered Rynlee and upset you, she's just so frustrated with herself." His eyes danced between mine. "What she did was terrible. Unforgivable. But, at the end of the day, Rynlee's okay, right? Nothing happened, thanks to you. We can't be mad at her forever."

"She knew, Jack. She had to have known."

He squeezed my hands, though I could see in his eyes he didn't believe me. Not fully, anyway. "I'm not saying you have to forgive her right away, or even completely ever, but…just…she *is* sorry, okay?"

I nodded and rolled over, feeling his hand leave my skin slowly. When he lowered his head onto the pillow, there was no anger in his sigh and there was no rage as he rolled to his side and flipped off the light. Jack was nothing like my ex, yet just as blinded by something he loved. For Travis, it was music. For Jack, apparently it was going to be his mother.

I didn't want to be *that* wife. I didn't want to make my husband choose between one side of his family and another, especially when I longed to have a family of my own. Especially when my parents weren't around and I'd never have to know the pain of choosing between a spouse and a parent. I loved him, and I needed this to work. I needed him to know I'd do anything to keep him, to keep our family together. But I couldn't pretend everything was okay.

How was I going to tell my husband I was pretty sure his mother had tried to kill our child?

CHAPTER FOURTEEN

LOREN

A few days later, after no further incident, I had convinced myself I'd overreacted. Was I really sure she knew about the peanut butter? I'd told her, but what if she was distracted? What if she truly didn't remember? She'd been nothing but kind since that day, and had even bought groceries to thank us for letting her stay. The night before, she'd surprised Rynlee with a coloring book and a new set of markers. I felt guilty for the harsh words—harsher thoughts—I'd had about Coralee, and I planned to tell her so the next time I saw her.

I pressed a pen of eyeliner to my eyelid, drawing a thin line. I jumped as my phone buzzed on the vanity. When I flipped it over to read the message on the screen, my stomach knotted immediately.

Meredith.

I opened the message, reading over the three short sentences repeatedly:

Will be gone longer...maybe much. I think I'm in love. How's the store? Xx.

How was I supposed to respond to that? I groaned, rubbing a finger in between my eyebrows to smooth the wrinkle I felt forming. Finally, I tapped the reply box and began to type.

Store's fine, but it's been a lot. We really need you ba—

No.

I erased it.

Meredith deserved happiness, she did. And if it truly was love, I didn't want to make her feel guilty for it. She'd always been my rock, there for me when I needed it. It seemed like it was my turn to return the favor.

Oooh, love, huh? I can't wait to meet him. Hope you're having fun. Store's fine, Becky's a lifesaver. We'll hold down the fort until you get back. Hope to see you soon. Xx.

With that, I placed the phone face down and swiped eyeliner across the other eyelid until they matched. When they did, I stood up, running a hand through my hair. *That'll do.*

I left my bedroom, listening carefully for noise downstairs as I made my way down the hall. Jack had already left for work and I hadn't heard a peep from Rynlee yet, so I'd need to wake her up soon. I needed to spend the next few days at the store for an entire shift. As amazing as Becky was, I couldn't keep relying on her to keep everything afloat. That wasn't her job, it was mine. Er, it was mine and Meredith's, but effectively mine for the foreseeable future.

When I stepped onto the hardwood of the first floor, I instantly knew something was wrong. Now that I was on the same level, Rynlee's quiet laughter could be heard coming from down the hall.

I looked around me, trying to determine where she was. "Rynlee?" I called.

The laughter immediately stopped. "Rynlee? Where are you?" I took a step toward the noise. Was it coming from the bathroom? The den?

Then, I heard hurried footsteps and I had my answer. *The office.*

I moved toward it quickly. Rynlee wasn't allowed in my office. It was where I kept all of our important documents, everything I needed for work. I swung the chestnut door open, my jaw dropping. "What did you do?" I asked, lowering myself to her level.

My daughter stood in front of me, her head hung down, three markers in each of her tiny hands. When I lifted her chin, her face was just as covered in ink as the rest of her. "Rynlee...why—?" I couldn't speak as I looked around my usually pristine office. Papers littered the floor, excel sheets and receipts covered in marker to the point that they'd become illegible, she'd drawn scribbly pictures all over the suede chair I'd had since she was a newborn, and the pictures I'd had hung on the wall—the business plans and family photos, were all torn down up to a certain height. Glass littered the floor where the frames had fallen. I looked back to my daughter in horror, her tiny, blue eyes already filled with tears.

"Why would you do this, baby?" I asked, my voice shaking as I tried to keep my anger in check. "You know you aren't allowed in Mommy's office. And who gave you markers? Those have to stay in the kitchen."

"I'm sorry, Mommy," she cried, no real answer given. Her rainbow fists balled up and she placed them over her eyes, falling into my arms and nearly knocking the two of us down. I placed one hand behind me to steady us and a piece of glass nicked my palm.

"It's okay," I said, patting her back as I scanned the room again. I placed my bleeding palm in my mouth, trying to stop the bleeding. *It's all just stuff. It can be fixed. It can be fixed. It can be fixed.* I repeated the mantra over and over, trying to remain calm when all I wanted to do was cry. How had this happened? I hadn't even known she was awake. My room was always the first place she went when she woke up. I pulled her away from my chest. "Why didn't you come wake me up, sweetheart? When you woke up, why didn't you come to Mommy's room?"

She frowned, still rubbing her eyes. "I don't know."

Okay, how about an easier one? "Who gave you markers?"

Her eyes went wide. "Ms. Coralee."

My suspicions were confirmed. I placed the markers on top of my desk and stood, lifting her with me. I had to go. I had to think. Angry, venom-filled thoughts raced through my mind. I shut the office door as we stepped out into the hall, unable to look at the mess waiting for me when I returned. I moved toward the living room, then the kitchen, and found Coralee exactly where I'd found her last time.

"Did you give Rynlee markers?" I asked my mother-in-law, her back to me as she flipped a pancake.

She spun around. "Yes, I—oh. Oh, God." She stared at my daughter's colorful arms, legs, and face. "Oh, no." Her frail, wrinkled fingers moved to her lips.

"She's not allowed to have markers unless someone's sitting with her at the table. She...destroyed my office."

"I don't know the rules of the house. I didn't even think... I'm not used to having a little one around." She paused. No apology. "I was trying to be nice. You were still in bed and she was bored." She gestured toward the pan. "I was even making her pancakes—no peanut butter, don't worry."

I sighed, bouncing her higher on my hip as her weight began to be too much. "It's fine, I just…okay." I couldn't think of anything else to say. Her excuse was believable enough, but I was still furious. Now I was going to end up late for work, and I wouldn't be able to leave until I'd cleaned my office, there was no question about that. I stepped back out of the kitchen and hurried down the hall, headed toward the bathroom.

"Are you mad at me, Mommy?" Rynlee asked as I pulled her clothes off.

"No, baby, I'm not mad at you. But you *do* know better than to color on anything but paper. And especially not anything in Mommy's office. Why would you do that?"

"I drew you a picture," she said, her tiny voice an octave higher than usual.

I huffed out a breath, hoisting her into the bath.

"Are you mad at Ms. Coralee?" she asked, sinking into the water and watching as the colors melted away almost instantly. I could only hope my office would do the same with a bit of soap and water, though I knew the papers wouldn't be salvageable.

"No, baby, I'm not mad at anyone."

"Mommy?" she said, glancing back at me worriedly.

"Yes?"

"You're bleeding."

I looked down at my hand, where her gaze led me, to see crescent moons carved into my palm. Seeing the wounds gave way for the pain to hit me. I shook my hand, reaching for some toilet paper to staunch it. "You're right, I am. It's okay, just a little blood." If I looked closely enough, I'd find little crescent moon scars in similar places on both palms, but it was a habit I thought I'd broken with the disappearance of Rynlee's father—the disappearance of my stress. It seemed there was a new stress in my life now. I'd have to do something about that.

CHAPTER FIFTEEN

LOREN

A few nights later, Jack and I both worked late. By the time I arrived home, Rynlee was fast asleep. I carried her from the car into the house, her body dead weight in my arms.

Coralee was sitting on the couch wearing an emerald green dress, her hair perfectly curled. She shot up at the sight of me, standing in my presence as I pictured her doing to her husband for so many years.

"What's the occasion?" I asked, eyeing her.

"No occasion," she told me. "I just wanted to get back to feeling like myself. I made dinner for you all. Lasagna." Her smile was tight, and I had a feeling she was going to ask me for a favor.

I looked around the house. "Where's Jack?"

"He just went up to take a shower. He'll be back down soon. Can I take something from you?" she asked, though she didn't extend her arms to match her words.

"No, that's okay," I said, probably too sharply. "I need to

get her laid down. We stopped and grabbed dinner on our way home."

"Oh," she said, her voice falling so much it made me feel guilty. Slightly guilty.

"I appreciate you making dinner, though, really. Jack should've told you. We typically eat out if both of us work late."

She jerked her head in what looked like a nod, but was too quick. "Of course. Not to worry, it'll keep. I'll go make Jack and me a plate, then."

I nodded, not wanting to point out that Jack had likely already eaten, too. Rynlee's weight was already too much, and I had a flight of stairs to make it up. "Good night, Coralee." I strode past her, making my way up the stairs and toward Rynlee's bedroom. I didn't bother changing her clothes—she was exhausted, as was I. Instead, I covered her up, kissed her forehead, then retreated to my own room, desperate to get out of my clothes.

I pushed the bedroom door open, smiling at Jack as he turned around, shock on his face as he attempted to cover himself with a towel.

"Well, hello handsome," I said, offering a half-laugh.

He gave me a lopsided grin, letting the towel fall away. "Hello, beautiful. How was your day?"

I winced. "I wish you hadn't asked."

His face went serious. "What do you mean?"

"I don't want to think about it right now," I said, climbing onto the bed on my knees and making my way toward him. I ran a finger down his still-wet chest. "I'd rather think about you, fresh out of the shower." I pressed my lips into his, one hand moving to the back of his neck. He groaned, falling to the bed on top of me as our kisses grew more passionate.

His hand slid up my side, his palms cool on my skin as his kisses moved to my neck. "I missed you," he whispered, his teeth grazing my ear.

"I missed you, too," I admitted, pulling him back to my lips. It had been so long since we'd had a moment to ourselves. It seemed that since the wedding, our alone time had been more scant than ever.

He rubbed his hand over my hair, his movements tender when I wanted passion. I bit his lip in between kisses, trying to steer him in the right direction. He pulled away, his brow raised teasingly.

"Feisty, huh?" He nipped at my lip, trailing his kisses across my jawline and down my chest until the fabric of my shirt stopped him. Instead of moving my shirt out of the way, he sat up. "To be continued, I'm afraid."

"Huh?" I asked, shocked back to reality.

"I have to go eat dinner with Mom," he said.

"Can't it wait?"

"I don't want to make her wait too long."

"No, just me, then?"

He kissed me again, trying to keep the peace, but I was no longer in the mood to be pleasant. "I won't keep you waiting long either."

"Didn't you already eat?" I asked, still pouting, as he pulled his pajama pants on. He grabbed a T-shirt out of the drawer and pulled it over his head.

"No, Mom called me and told me not to because she was cooking for us, didn't she call you?"

"Seriously?" I asked, propping myself up on my elbows.

"Yeah, I told her we always eat out when we work late, and she said she'd call you."

"She didn't."

He looked toward our door, his brows drawn together in confusion. "Hm. Sorry, babe. It must've slipped her mind."

"Yeah, right."

"What's that mean?" he asked, slight frustration in his voice.

"Just that I don't think any of this is an accident, Jack. I can't believe you can look at me with a straight face and say you do. She's never been nice to me, she tried to poison Rynlee, today she gave her markers and let her destroy my office—"

"She *what?*"

"Yeah, when I woke up, Rynlee had colored all over my office, furniture included. I took pictures." I reached for my phone to show him the devastation. "She broke picture frames, too. There was a lot of important stuff in there that's ruined."

He scrolled through the pictures with his thumb before handing it back to me. "Did you get it cleaned up?"

"Yeah, but it made me three hours late for work, and there's still a lot I have to do. The chair is completely ruined."

"Did you ask Mom about it? Are you sure she's the one who gave her the markers? Maybe Rynlee got into them on her own—"

"Yes, I asked. She told me she was. I'm half-convinced she put her in the office as well."

He cocked his head to the side, his expression full of disbelief. "You can't be serious."

"I am, Jack. I think she's doing every bit of this on purpose, including leaving me and Rynlee out of dinner plans."

"Oh, come on, Lor."

"Come on, what?"

"She's not doing that on purpose. She's not *evil*, she's just...grieving. She's probably not thinking clearly with so much on her mind. She told me she's really enjoying her time here. I can't thank you enough for letting her stay."

I stared at him. Was he right? Was I going crazy with suspicion? Truth was, I couldn't be sure.

Before I could respond, he spoke again. "This is hard on all of us, you know? It's not like I planned for this to be the start of our marriage."

"How much longer will she be staying?" I asked the question that could solve everything.

"I have no idea," he said, then, when I frowned, he added, "not too much longer, I'm sure."

I nodded. "Okay."

"Can we just make the best of it, please?"

"Okay."

He stepped back toward the door cautiously. "Okay." His next sentence was spoken as a question. "I love you?"

"I love you, too," I confirmed. I loved him enough to protect him from whatever monster we'd let into our home.

I HADN'T BEEN asleep for long when a knock rang out on the door. I shot up. "Rynlee?" It wasn't like her to knock, but maybe now that Jack lived here she would.

"No," the voice answered, and Jack popped his head in, flipping on the light. I rubbed the sleep from my eyes. "Shoot, sorry, babe. I didn't think you'd be asleep yet. I can come back."

"No, it's okay. I just dozed off. What are you—"

Taking me at my word, he pushed the door open wider,

the answer to my question stopping my words short. Coralee stood behind him, her hands clasped together in front of her stomach. She was still wearing the green evening gown.

"Loren, Jack's told me you're still upset about some of my behavior since I've moved in." She looked to Jack, her voice mockingly feeble. "I wanted you to know I never meant to upset you or Rynlee." I rubbed my eyes again, sitting up. Was I dreaming?

She stepped further into the room. "Jack, she was asleep," she said, apparently just realizing it. "Maybe we should come back."

"She said it's okay," Jack said, nodding at me. "Just tell her, Mom."

"Tell me, what?"

"Tell you that...I'm...I'm incredibly embarrassed about my behavior since I moved in. I don't remember you telling me about the peanut butter, but obviously if you had, I shouldn't have tried to serve it to Rynlee. And today with the markers, it was a mistake that I take full responsibility for. I'm still learning the rules here, and I thought the child was old enough to know better. I'll know from now on. And as far as dinner tonight, Jack *did* tell me to call you and warn you about dinner, but I was just pulling into the store, and I'd planned to call you when I got out. Obviously, that didn't happen. It's all been a misunderstanding, and I hope you can see that. I'm very grateful for you allowing me to stay here, and I'd never want to make you think otherwise."

She stopped, her gaze locked on the floor as she waited for me to respond. "It's okay, Coralee. Honestly. I'm just... Rynlee is all I have. I have to protect her. And this has been an adjustment, for all of us, I'm sure. But we're happy to have you here while you need us." I made sure to add that last sentence, because it wasn't permanent. It needed to end soon.

Jack looked smugly pleased, standing just behind Coralee, and I knew he thought it was resolved. But he hadn't heard what I had. There'd been no apology in her words, just an explanation.

I wanted to offer her an apology of my own: *I'm sorry you couldn't stay longer.*

CHAPTER SIXTEEN

LOREN

"Mom." The hurried whispers carried across the bedroom, rousing me from sleep. I felt her tiny hands on my face, fingers like ice against my skin. "Mom, wake up."

I jolted awake then, realizing it wasn't a dream. Rynlee stood in front of me, her hair messy from sleep, eyes wide.

"What is it, sweetheart? Are you okay?" I sat up in bed, looking her over thoroughly.

She shook her head, pushing herself further toward me so I would lift her into our bed. Jack stirred beside me, looking over. "What's going on?" he asked, his deep voice coated with sleep.

I looked at Rynlee, still waiting for the answer.

Her voice was quieter than usual when she spoke, the fear in it evident. "Someone's in my room."

My blood ran cold as I heard the words, my body growing rigid. "What do you mean?" I asked, trying to keep my voice calmer than I felt.

"Someone's in my room," she repeated.

"Someone who?" Jack sat up finally, his voice authoritative as he lifted the blankets from his legs and climbed from bed, still a bit woozy with sleep.

"I don't know," she answered.

"Did you see someone in there, Ryn? Who was it? How did you get up here?"

"They were just making noise," she said, her tone telling me it should've been obvious. "In my closet and stuff. Like... growling and scratching."

"Growling and scratching? Who's *they*, Ryn?" I asked, but Jack wasn't waiting for any further explanation.

"Stay here," he warned, pointing a finger at me. "You have your phone?"

"I do," I said, glancing at it across the room where it charged. "Should I call nine-one-one?"

"Let me go check it out first. It could just be a mouse or something. But you two stay in here. Keep your phone with you...just in case." In case of what, he didn't say, but the weight of his words sat heavy in the room.

I nodded. "Okay...be careful." I wanted to stop him, make him stay with me, hidden away from the danger until we could get the police there. But another part of me believed the danger couldn't be real. It was an old house, after all. It wasn't uncommon for us to find mice lurking in the lesser-used rooms.

He stepped out into the hall without a weapon, and I pulled my daughter into my chest, holding her tighter than ever as I listened to the deafening silence, waiting to hear something—anything—that would give me a clue as to what was going on.

We waited, Rynlee's tiny hands on my arms as I held her, our breaths syncing. Every pop or creak of the house, the usual noises it made—the foundation settling, the pipes rattling—caused me to jump. Rynlee sat quietly, her eyes plastered on the door as mine were. I wanted to assure her everything would be all right, to give her peace even when I felt I had none, but I couldn't move.

Creeeeeaaakk.

Someone was coming down the hall.

I shoved the covers from our legs, clamping a hand over her mouth and whispering, "Shh," in her ear as we moved across the floor quietly.

This was it.

This was really happening.

I grabbed the phone from the table against the wall, dialing 9-1-1 and hovering my finger above the green button that would initiate the call. We moved across the floor slowly, our movements silent, and I thanked God for my obedient child at that moment.

We sank into the walls of the closet and I pulled the doors shut, feeling her shaking in my arms. She looked at me, her eyes wide with questions she couldn't ask. I kissed her forehead, listening.

Listening.

Listening.

My heart pounded in my chest, my ears burning hot. I wiped sweat from my brow, an action that was useless since my palms were slick with sweat, too. My breathing was too loud as I tried to listen. Had I imagined the noise?

Just when I thought maybe that was the case, I heard it again.

Creeeeaaakk.

Then again, *creeeeaaakk.* Someone was definitely out there. But what were they doing? And where was Jack?

I sucked in a haggard breath, placing a hand to my chest in an effort to quiet my racing heart. I couldn't think, couldn't catch my breath. The ice cold fear was overtaking me.

I lifted Rynlee, placing her on my pile of shoes in the back of my closet and pushing her back as far as I could. I put my fingers to my lips, telling her to keep silent as I moved a suitcase and an old comforter in front of her. Somehow, my body knew what to do while my mind panicked.

I moved to the front of the closet, peering through the crack in the doors. From there, I had a decent view of the bedroom door. It was still shut, and no one had come for us. Not yet, anyway.

I heard Rynlee shift in place, and I knew the shoes weren't the most comfortable seat. What was I supposed to do? There was nothing there to protect us? I looked down at my phone, the screen black from lack of use.

Just then, the door opened quickly, and I jolted, letting out a squeak of fear.

Jack looked around, flipping on the light. "Lor?"

I reached behind me, pulling Rynlee out of her hiding spot and wiping away the fresh tears that broke my heart as I shoved open the closet door. "What is it? Is everything okay?"

He nodded, taking in our frazzled appearance and wrapping his arms around us. "Everything's fine. There was nothing there. It must've been the wind that she heard. It sounds like a pretty serious storm is coming."

"I heard someone walk past our door," I said, begging him to calm my fears.

"It was me," he said. "I went up to Mom's room and made sure she was okay."

"And she was?"

He nodded. "Sound asleep in her bed. I hardly woke her to check her room."

"But you did check it?"

"I checked everywhere," he said. "No one's here. It was just the wind."

I looked to Rynlee then, kissing her head and smoothing her hair. "Did you hear that? It was just the wind, sweetie. Everything's okay."

"Okay," she said, trusting us fully, while I wished I could do the same.

"Do you want to stay here with us tonight?" I asked, looking at Jack who nodded in confirmation.

She tucked her head into my neck. "Yes."

We climbed into bed then and Jack flipped off the light, shutting the door firmly before he made his way to the bed.

An hour passed, with me staring at the ceiling and listening to the slow breathing of Rynlee first, then Jack. I couldn't sleep; I wasn't sure I'd ever sleep again.

As much as I wanted to believe him, Rynlee had never heard noises at night, not even on the stormiest night. Try as I might to deny it, I had a suspicion gnawing at me that whatever she'd heard, wasn't just the wind.

THE NEXT MORNING, I jumped out of bed well before either of our alarms had gone off. It's not like it mattered. Like I'd predicted, I hadn't slept a wink. Jack and Rynlee were still sound asleep, and I left them with one last glance cast their way, heading down the hall and toward her room. I wanted to see for myself just what had caused my child to be so upset.

I opened her bedroom door slowly, half expecting someone to jump out and grab me. My hand felt along the wall for her light switch, connecting with it quickly and flipping it on. I stared around the room, looking for some sort of clue. As I moved across the carpet, my breathing quiet, I studied the space I'd spent so much time in with Rynlee. It was a space I was familiar with, yet something felt odd. There was a strangeness in the air I couldn't quite put my finger on. I spun around in my spot, trying to decide what was wrong. It was almost as if everything had been moved, but only slightly. Before, I was sure the tiny pink recliner she'd gotten for her third birthday had sat slightly to the left of her small, white bookshelf, but now it sat to the right. Had Rynlee moved it? It was a possibility, I supposed. But why? And why, now, was her night light in a wall plate where I'd not placed it? Maybe Sarah had moved it, or Meredith, but I couldn't recall seeing it there yesterday.

I was more suspicious that day, looking more closely, I reminded myself. I was looking for something off, so if anything was I was sure to find it. But it could've been off for days, weeks even. It didn't prove anything.

I walked into her closet, looking around the walk-in. It was nearly the size of her room, just like the closet in my room, and also like the closet in my room, it was filled with a built-in bookcase and totes of old clothes and toys she'd outgrown. Her clothes had been shifted on the rack, everything pushed to one side. That definitely wasn't how it had been yesterday. Something was off. I couldn't decide what, and I had no proof. I knew after our last conversation, I would have to be careful what I mentioned to Jack. He didn't believe me about Coralee, didn't believe me about something strange going on, so how could I approach him with this without having anything solid to show him?

"Everything okay?" I jumped at the sound of his voice, looking over my shoulder with a hand clasped to my mouth. "Sorry, didn't mean to scare you."

"That's okay," I said, trying to catch my breath. "I was just checking her room to make sure everything looked okay."

He nodded, one side of his mouth drawn up as he let out a yawn. "Anything out of place?"

"Nothing's jumping out at me right away," I said. I was desperate to tell him what I'd noticed, but I knew it would be brushed aside.

He glanced down the hall where Rynlee's footsteps could be heard. "She's in here," he told her, then looked at me. "We had a bet about whether you were in the bathroom or kitchen. Guess neither of us won." He scooped her up, passing her toward me.

"Good morning, princess," I said, kissing her face. "Did you sleep okay?"

She nodded. "Mommy?"

"What is it, sweet girl?"

"Can I sleep with you from now on? In case the monsters come back?"

I looked at Jack. He narrowed his eyes at me, his lips a thin line as he shook his head ever so slightly. "Rynlee, there are no monsters, sweetheart. You know that." He was passing her comments off as childish nonsense, but I believed her. I held her cheek to mine, closing my eyes.

"We'll have to see, baby. But I promise you I won't let anyone hurt you, okay? Mommy and Jack will scare away any monsters," I said, hoping to ease her fears more than he had.

She smiled slightly, her fears eased for the moment, though mine weighed in my chest, more real than ever.

CHAPTER SEVENTEEN

LOREN

When dinner time came that night, I was no more at ease than I had been that morning, despite my growing exhaustion. I'd taken the afternoon off to be with Rynlee, and she and I had spent the day painting a new canvas that I was excited to hang in my office. It was my way of helping her feel more secure, while also allowing her to help redecorate the office.

I pulled Coralee's leftover lasagna out of the oven, my stomach growling as I watched the cheese bubble.

"Ryn, wash up, Jack will be home soon," I told her, scooting the stool toward the sink so she could climb up and wash her hands. I hit the home button on my phone, checking to see if I had any new messages from him.

Coralee, like usual, had stayed in her room for most of the day. All the better for us, honestly. Even though she lived under our roof, it was so rare that I saw her it was almost hard to remember she was there sometimes.

"I'm going to go tell Ms. Coralee supper is done, okay? You wash your hands, and I'll be right back."

"But, Mommy, don't leave me," she begged, her eyes wide with fear.

"Okay, okay." I rushed toward her, angry with myself for not thinking. It was obvious what had happened wasn't going away any time soon. Try as Jack might to explain it away, Rynlee had been really affected by it. I stood by her side while she scrubbed her hands, before drying them on her pants.

Together, we made our way up the stairs and toward Coralee's room. When we arrived on the third floor, I perked my nose toward the air. *What is that?*

I moved quicker, hoping the smell would fade, but it only grew stronger as we neared Coralee's door. I knew the smell well; my father had smoked for years before eventually quitting. Still, that didn't stop him from passing away from lung cancer after ten years without a cigarette.

"Coralee?" I called, rapping on the door. Jack had never mentioned her smoking, and he knew how I felt about it. Surely he'd mentioned to her she couldn't smoke in the house. "Coralee, are you in there?" I called again, knocking louder.

When she didn't answer, I twisted the knob, taking in a breath as I stared around an almost unrecognizable room. The wallpaper I'd meticulously pasted on the walls, after picking it out and having it shipped from a small shop across the country, was completely gone, while fresh yellow paint adorned the walls. The bed, which had once been directly in front of me, had been pushed against the wall to my left. The room reeked of paint and cigarette smoke, Coralee's clothes were strewn about, empty plates of rotting food lying here and there. I covered my mouth, nearing tears as I realized there was a red wine stain on the antique quilt that had been handed down from my mother's grand-mother. She'd apparently taken it upon herself to remove it from the quilt rack on the wall and place it on the bed. I moved toward it, a mixture of anger and nausea filling my belly as I lifted it up. There was a cigarette burn near the edge.

"What the hell do you think you're doing?" I heard the vile voice demand. I spun around to face her, holding out the quilt. I had no idea what to ask her about first.

"What have you done?" I asked, gesturing around the room. My hands shook with anger, my throat tight. "Why would you do this?"

Her eyes didn't follow my gaze around the room. Instead she remained locked on me. "Why would you come into my room without my permission?"

"I knocked, Coralee. I knocked, and you didn't answer." I felt my face grow hot with anger, my vision nearly blurring I was so angry. I wasn't sure whether to cry or throw up.

"I was in the restroom," she said, matter-of-factly, still not answering my question.

"Why would you paint this room? Or move things around? This is *not* okay." I was shaking with anger, holding the quilt in one hand, my daughter's hand in the other. "This was my great grandmother's quilt. It's too old to be used."

"Jack told me to make myself comfortable." Her cold, dead stare burned into me, her indifference causing my anger to swell.

"That doesn't mean *paint* the room! That doesn't mean redecorate. You are our guest, Coralee. Your time here is temporary. You aren't allowed to just do as you see fit with a home that isn't yours." My chest constricted with my screams, my anger rising to new levels. I felt my nails digging into my palms, knowing that if I looked down, I'd surely see blood beading on the broken skin.

She was silent, her chest rising and falling with heavy breaths and she stared me down.

"The wallpaper here cost a fortune. And...have you been smoking?"

"My husband just died, Loren. Perhaps you forget."

I huffed out a breath. "*Perhaps* I don't forget, Coralee. And I am sorry for your loss, but that doesn't give you the right to do this. Any of this. You are not to do anything else to this house, or this room. You are not to smoke in my house. I won't allow it. And *please* ask before you help yourself to my family heirlooms."

"You'll do well not to speak to me that way. I am not your child, Loren, and I *will* be respected."

"I tried. I tried to respect you, I tried to make you feel welcome, but this...this has gone too far." I felt tears stinging my eyes again, my whole body trembling with fury. "I'll ask Jack to take you back to your home. Tonight. I'm sorry...this just isn't going to work."

To my surprise, her lips curled up into a slight smile. "Very well."

I jerked my head back, trying to read her expression, though it sent chills right through me. Perhaps she didn't believe me. I didn't care. She needed to know I was serious. "He'll be home soon. You should pack your things."

"I'll get right on it," she said, making no move to do as I'd said.

Rynlee was staring up at me with wide eyes, and as much as I wanted to stay and enforce my words, I had to leave. I made a point of leaving the door open as we left, clutching the quilt as if it were a lifeline.

I hoped and prayed Jack would agree with me, that he would see how wrong she'd been in her choices. There was no way I could forgive her for this. Not now. Possibly not ever.

I heard the front door open as we descended the stairs. At the same time, I heard a door slam up above me. Coralee had shut her door.

CHAPTER EIGHTEEN

LOREN

I approached Jack with a lump in my throat, hardly able to hold myself together. His smile faded quickly when he saw me and saw the distress on my face.

"Ryn, can you go over to your easel and draw Mommy a picture before dinner?"

"But I already washed my hands," she argued.

"It's okay, sweetheart," I said, giving her a nudge. She seemed unsure, but eventually gave in and made her way across the living room toward her easel and pulled out a coloring book, casting glances our way continuously to make sure we were still there. Merlin lay at her feet, yawning lazily.

"What happened?" he asked, looking down at the blanket. "Did she get paint on it?"

"No," I told him. "Have you...have you seen what your mother's done upstairs?"

His eyes traveled toward the stairs. "What do you mean? What's she done?"

"I don't...I don't even know where to begin. She painted the walls—"

"She *what?*" He moved like he was going to go upstairs to her, but turned back around to me. "Are you serious?"

"Yes, she painted, and rearranged the furniture. And she's been *smoking* up there. The room's a disaster. She took my great-grandmother's quilt," I held it out toward him, "off the wall and spilled red wine on it and left cigarette burns on it."

He seemed speechless as her offenses rolled off my tongue. When I was finished, he rubbed his jaw. "I can't believe she'd do that. Loren, I'm—I'm so sorry. What can I do?" His eyes danced between meeting mine and looking at the staircase. "Let me talk to her. I'll...I'll fix this."

"That wallpaper was original. It cost me a fortune. The room can be put back to normal as far as the furniture, and the smell can be aired out...eventually. But the paint, we can't fix that. And I'm not sure there's anything I can do to repair the holes in the quilt, even if by some miracle I can get the stains out. I'm sorry, Jack, I've tried...I've tried to be reasonable. I'm just not sure what else I can do. I can't put up with anything else."

"What are you saying?" His face grew instantly serious.

I sighed. "I've asked her to pack her things. I think it's time for her to go home."

"You're...kicking her out?"

"Jack, I need you to back me up on this. I've tried to be hospitable. I've tried to make her feel welcome, but it's just thing after thing that she's done. One issue after the next and, I'm sorry, but this draws the line. Who comes to stay at a person's house and paints the room they are in? It's...it's crazy."

I was staring at him, begging him to agree with me, but I couldn't read his stony-faced expression.

"I know she's been difficult and, honestly, for the life of me, I can't imagine what she was thinking with the paint. But, I'm sure she didn't realize the quilt was important to you. She probably just grew chilly. And...she's going through a lot, Lor. But if you just give me a chance to talk to her, I'll make sure she understands how serious this all was. I can fix this. I promise you I can if you'll just give me a chance. My dad just died, sweetheart. She just lost the love of her life. I can't imagine how I'd feel if that was you...and we've not even been married a year. Imagine thirty-five." He pulled me in for a hug. "I'm just so sorry, Lor. Can we...can we take the quilt to have it repaired? Surely we can find someone."

"I'm sorry your dad died, Jack. I am. But that can't keep being the excuse we use to put aside all she's done. It can't. This is too much." I pushed away from him, too angry for comfort. He needed to see reason.

"You don't know what it's like to—"

"I don't know what it's like to...to what, Jack? To lose someone important to me? My parents died. The man I planned to raise my child with walked out. I know what it's like to lose people. I know what pain feels like, but that doesn't give her or me or anyone else the right to destroy the property, or lives, of anyone else."

"She's *destroying* your life now?" he asked, an edge to his tone. He folded his arms over his chest, raising a palm to rub his jaw. "It's...it's a quilt, Loren. And wallpaper. Things that can be fixed or replaced. This is my mother. I'm willing to call her out. What she's done is wrong, and I won't let her get away with it, but throwing her out seems extreme. You know how close we are." I thought of the wedding night then, fresh anger filling me.

"Yes, you've made that abundantly clear."

"You don't know what it'll do to me to have to ask her to leave. Please just...let her have a bit more time."

I picked at a piece of skin around my fingernails, staring at the dried blood on my palms. "Jack, I don't want to fight with you, but...can't you see what this is doing to us? To me?"

"You know, I never took you as a selfish person, Loren, but right now...I'm really not liking this version of you. She's my mother—"

"I tried—"

"Did you?" he asked, his voice too loud. Rynlee spun around to look at us, shocked by his outburst. He smiled at her, as did I, assuring her everything was fine. When she turned back to her art, he lowered his voice. "I don't feel like you've given her a fair chance to fit in here. She stays hidden because she's scared to do something wrong and upset you. I know it was your house before, Loren, but isn't it *our* house now? Don't I get a say in this?"

I frowned. Technically, yes, he was right. It was his house, too. I don't know why I'd never thought of it that way, the idea of splitting the only thing I'd ever truly owned terrified me, but I couldn't argue.

He stepped toward me. "I'll talk to her, okay? I'll fix the wallpaper, reorder it and install it myself if I have to. I'll talk to her about the smoking, and I'll find the best *quilt-fixer* there is," he smiled, trying to get me to smile back, but I refused, "to repair your grandmother's quilt. We'll fix this, but I just...I can't ask her to leave right now. I'm sorry. I'm asking you, as your husband, to give her a bit more time."

He said he was asking, but we both knew it wasn't a question. The argument was over. I nodded, not meeting his eyes, though I could feel his stare burning into me.

"Fine. But, Jack, if she does anything else—" I hated myself for agreeing, but as I stared past him, toward Rynlee, I knew I needed to keep things peaceful if at all possible. I needed a happy husband, a happy father for her. Coralee's presence in our home wasn't permanent. Soon, she'd be out of our hair, and I needed to keep my marriage strong for when that time came.

"She won't. I swear. I'm going to address this right now." He touched my arm, letting me know this wasn't a fight, and walked past me toward the stairs. When he was gone, I felt new tears in my eyes as I looked toward my daughter.

What had I done to our once peaceful lives for the sake of love? I'd promised myself my next relationship, my marriage, would be permanent. It would last, if not for my own happiness, then for Rynlee's. My little girl loved Jack. I loved Jack. I could make peace for the next few days. Ride out the storm.

Still, a question echoed in my head, taunting me. *What do I really know about this family?*

CHAPTER NINETEEN

LOREN

That night, Rynlee slept in between us, her eyes fluttering with peaceful dreams. Despite not having slept much the night before, I couldn't bring myself to drift off.

After a few desperate hours, I found myself wondering again about Rynlee's room. What had I missed? What was the feeling I couldn't seem to shake—that I'd overlooked something important, that there was something disturbing going on just under my nose. I couldn't simply disregard the fact that my daughter, who'd never been one to wake in the middle of the night due to nightmares or strange noises, was now too afraid to be left alone in a house she'd grown up in just weeks after my mother-in-law moved in.

Odd, at best, but I suspected there was more to it. I didn't trust Coralee. That was the bottom line, and I was determined to prove to Jack I was right about her. I needed to catch her in the act of doing something unforgivable and unexplainable—unlike the markers or even the cookies. He'd found so much to reason in her guilt, able to push most everything off on that, but I knew eventually she'd slip up, and when she did, I'd be there to catch her in the act. I held onto that hope to keep me sane.

I pushed the covers from my legs, not entirely sure where I was headed until I arrived at my daughter's door. I stepped into the room, the temperature a bit warmer than the hall, and stared around in the darkness. I moved around the room, looking for anything new out of place, but didn't see anything strange.

What did she hear? The answer had to be there.

I sat down on the edge of her bed, pulling the comforter back and sliding down under the covers. Her pillow was smaller than mine, with less support, so my head sank down practically to the mattress, and I made a mental note to buy her a new one soon.

My breaths came quickly, the sound like white noise in my ears as I stared at the ceiling of her room, willing the noise to come again. Was it possible we had a mouse? I reasoned that it wasn't *im*possible. We'd had them before. In a house as old as ours, it was a full-time job keeping them out, but I hadn't seen one yet that year.

If it were a mouse, just hearing its noises would've calmed my nerves, I was sure. I wanted the noise to be explainable. I wanted to hear an owl, or the wind blowing a tree branch into her window. I wanted it to be nothing.

For the longest time, it was literally that. Nothing. Silence. The sound of the heat kicking on, drowning out any chance of hearing anything else.

When I finally heard it, it roused me from sleep, though I hadn't realized I'd finally dozed off. My eyes darted open, but I didn't dare move any other part of me. Ice cold fear shot through me like lightning.

Scraaaaaatch.

Scraaaaatch.

Scraaaaaatch.

The noise whined above me, the unmistakable sound of scratching against wood. A tool of some kind. The noise was coming from directly above my head—Coralee's room.

I threw the covers back, stepping out of bed. *What the hell is she doing?* I darted from the room, hurrying down the hall and up the stairs before she had a chance to stop.

I grabbed for the golden handle, shoving her door open as quickly as I'd arrived to it, without a knock for a warning. I didn't want to give her the chance to stop whatever it was she was doing.

To my surprise, the room was dark, lit only by a small lamp near the bed. Coralee was sitting in an old rocker, a book in her hand, glasses balanced on the end of her nose, though her eyes were on me rather than the book.

"What on earth are you doing?" she asked, not moving out of her seat. I looked around the room—to my surprise, she'd arranged the furniture back to the way I'd had it, though the yellow paint and horrid smell weren't gone.

"Did you hear that noise?" I demanded.

"The polite thing to do before entering a bedroom, is knock, Loren." She set her book down on the nightstand beside her and pulled the glasses from her face. "I'd appreciate it if you'd start doing that."

"Aren't you going to answer me?"

"Aren't you going to start respecting my privacy?" There was a crooked, slight grin on her face. She was enjoying this. She was enjoying my slow descent into madness.

"Coralee, whatever issue you have with me, your games are scaring my daughter. Rynlee has nothing to do with this."

"I have no idea what you're talking about," she said simply. "Shut the door on your way out."

"I'm not leaving until you tell me what your plan is here. Why are you being so horrible to us? Why do you hate me?" I demanded, my lack of sleep speaking for me. "What have I ever done to you?"

She offered a loud laugh, and I heard footsteps headed our direction. Heavy footsteps. Jack's footsteps. "What were you doing up here? What was that noise?" I demanded, knowing my time was running up. She could see it too, I could tell. When she answered, her voice was slow and methodical.

"I didn't hear a thing."

Jack was up the stairs and coming down the hall, rubbing sleep from his worried eyes. To my relief, Rynlee wasn't with him.

"What are you doing? Is everything okay?" he asked, looking at me, and then, when he grew closer, at his mother.

"Ask your wife," Coralee answered. "She just barged into my room without so much as a knock. Scared me half to death."

"Is that true?" Jack asked, looking at me with dread.

"I...well, yes, but...I stayed in Rynlee's room for a while, trying to see if I'd hear the noise again."

"You what? I told you it was just—"

"It wasn't, Jack! I heard it again, and it was loud. A loud scraping noise. Coming from this room." I looked at Coralee, daring her to explain. "She's trying to scare Rynlee."

"What are you talking about? Why would she want to do that? It could've been anything, Loren. You can't just go around—"

Scraaaaatch.

Scraaaaatch.

Scraaaaatch.

The conversation halted as our attention was drawn back to my mother-in-law. Her icy gray eyes bore into mine, her hands folded across her chest as she pushed the rocking chair with her feet, the bottom scraping the hardwood floor and recreating a sound much like the one I'd heard.

"Was...this the sound?" she asked, feigning innocence.

I stared at her, listening to the moan of the rocker as it moved, my eyes blinking back unexpected tears.

"Was it?" Jack asked when I didn't answer right away.

"I'm sorry if I was scaring little Rynlee. I didn't think about it. I'm...well, it's embarrassing to admit, but I'm having trouble sleeping at night without Malcolm, so I've stayed up reading. The rocking motion calms me, but I can stop if it's disturbing you."

I bit the inside of my cheek, fury filling me, though I couldn't let it show. She'd known exactly what she was doing. I could see it in the way her face changed when Jack was no longer looking at her. This was a game, and she was playing her hand all too well.

"Is that what you were hearing, Loren?" Jack asked again.

"Possibly, but I can't be sure," I said, and it was true. The noise had seemed much louder from the quiet bedroom below, but that didn't mean anything necessarily. Sound traveled weirdly through our old house, always had. Some rooms seemed paper thin, while others were basically soundproof.

Jack, seeming to understand, put a hand on my back. "Mom, do you mind not doing that? Your room is right above Rynlee's, and it does seem to be frightening her."

She smiled dotingly at him. "Of course, dear. I'm sorry about that."

He nodded, believing it was done. "Right. Now, that's settled. Everybody happy? Sorry to disturb you, Mom. We'll just go to bed."

I took an even breath to try and stay calm, frustrated that she always seemed able to explain away her crimes.

"That's quite all right, dear," she said, though she stood as we began to leave. "I know you'll do whatever it takes to protect Rynlee." Her gaze caused mine to falter slightly as she moved toward us. "I would do the same for my child. It's a mother's love. I *am* sorry for disturbing her, though, and I'll try to keep it down when it's this late." I turned, walking out of the room with Jack's insistent hand on my back. "But, Loren?" she said, causing me to look back at her. "Next time, you *will* knock, won't you?" There was a smile on her face, one that I knew Jack was buying into completely, but I saw the evil behind the mask. She shut the door without waiting for my answer, and I heard a swift *click* letting me know she'd locked it behind her.

CHAPTER TWENTY

LOREN

Need to talk to you. Please call me when you get a chance.

I sent the text to Meredith the next morning when I arrived at the store. As much as I didn't want to bother her, I needed to talk to someone who I knew would be on my side. No matter what, Meredith would know what to do. In every situation of my life, she'd been the advice-giver, and without her, I felt lost.

I unbuckled Rynlee from her car seat and carried her into the building, her little arms wrapped tightly around my neck.

"Hey, stranger,'" Becky said, a giant smile on her face when we walked through the door. "Nice to see you here."

"Hey," I said. "I brought you coffee." I held out the tray in my hands, letting her take it before I set Rynlee on the floor. She took off instantly.

"Thanks," Becky said, taking the cup. "Hey, listen…I need to talk to you."

My heart fell at the words, knowing what they would mean. "You're leaving."

Instead of shaking her head, dismissing the ridiculous claim, she pressed her lips together. "I'm sorry, I know this is the worst possible time."

I tried not to let her see my hands beginning to shake. "I, uh, no. Well, yes, because any time would be awful to lose you, but it'll be okay. How long do I have you?"

"A month," she said, a bit of relief in her eyes. "Maybe a bit more. Jude's getting transferred to the Cincinnati office."

"Cincinnati?" I asked, my jaw dropping. "Wow! Long way from home. Are you guys...excited...nervous..." I trailed off, waiting for her to fill in the blank.

She patted the counter, a growing smile on her face. "Excited, mostly, but nervous, too. Neither of us have ever been more than a few hours away from this place. It's going to be a big change."

I walked around the edge of the counter, holding my arms out to hug her despite the gripping fear in my belly. *What am I going to do without her?* "I'm so happy for you," I told her.

"Thanks," she said, patting my back before pulling out of the hug. "I just feel so guilty. I've been avoiding saying anything because I know how much you have on your plate right now, but I wanted to give you as much time as possible to prepare." She paused, biting her lip. "Meredith will be back by then, right? I mean, I won't be leaving you all alone?" Her sentence was a question, one I desperately wished I knew the answer to.

"I hope so," I said, "but don't worry about it. We'll figure something out, if not. Do you think you could get a 'Help Wanted' sign put up in the window for me here in the next day or two? Hopefully we can get someone hired and trained by you before you leave."

She nodded. "I'd be happy to."

"Thanks, Becky," I said with a small sigh. I didn't want her to feel guilty. Honestly, I didn't. We were paying her minimum wage, and she was a sweet girl with her life ahead of her. I wanted her to move on and live her life, despite the position that would put me in. I looked over my shoulder to where Ryn stood, smelling each individual flower in the shop. "I'm going to step into the office and check some emails. Do you need anything from me?"

"Nope," Becky said, and I watched her shoulders fall with relief as I walked past her.

"Rynlee, Mommy's going into the office. You can come in here if you want."

"Okay," she called loudly, though she didn't follow me. I hadn't expected her to. From the time Meredith and I had signed a lease on the shop, it had become Rynlee's favorite place. She'd grown up there just as much as she had our home.

At least one of those places still felt safe.

When I sat down in my chair in the small office, I felt my phone vibrate in my jacket pocket. I pulled it out.

What is the matter?

Thank God, it was Meredith. I dialed her number, desperate to hear her voice. To my surprise, it rang through to voicemail. I frowned, typing out a message.

Can I call you? Long story.

The bubbles came up quickly, letting me know she was typing. I waited anxiously, wondering why she hadn't just called me back. I tried to keep the irritation at bay.

Can't talk right now, we're in the mountains and don't have service. Just text. What's going on?

In the mountains? I furrowed my brow. **Becky put in her**

130

notice. I decided to tell her. **So we need to figure out what we're going to do about hiring someone new. Do you have any idea how long you'll be gone?**

This time, the bubbles didn't appear right away, and a nagging sense of dread filled my stomach. I watched the screen for a few moments, waiting for her answer and tapping my pen against the desk with irritation. Why was this all on me? I'd tried my hardest to be understanding and supportive, but why was I the one left to deal with everyone else's issues? It just didn't seem fair.

My phone dinged in response. **He is taking me to Spain soon. I am not sure when I will be back. Can you handle it?**

I sighed. I wanted to tell her that of course I couldn't handle it, that when we'd agreed to go into business together, we'd agreed to handle everything equally, that this was just as much her problem as it was mine, and that she was incredibly selfish for disappearing and leaving me without so much as a goodbye. I wanted her to know how much she'd hurt me, on top of all the pain I was already feeling, but I couldn't. I couldn't say any of that. Instead, I said, **Sounds good. I'll figure something out. I wanted to talk to you about something else too...I need advice.**

This time, her response was instant. **What's going on?**

It's about Jack, I said. **His mother has moved in with us and we've been having issues.**

Uh-oh, trouble in paradise? Why's his mother there?

I sighed, resigning myself to the fact that this conversation was going to have to happen via text. **Jack's father passed away right after the wedding and she's having a hard time...supposedly.**

Supposedly? She was texting back faster than ever now,

making me question her *stuck in the mountains* excuse. Maybe she was just tired of listening to my problems now that she had her own life.

I'm just not sure I believe it. She's been really difficult and Jack doesn't see it. It's just making me uncomfortable.

So, kick her out? It's your house, Lor. You make the rules.

It's not that simple. I rolled my eyes, *if only.* If I were Meredith, it would be that simple, no question, but I hadn't been blessed with the backbone my cousin had.

Why not?

Because Jack's my husband now, I have to consider his feelings. He wants her there.

Sounds like Mommy-issues to me. I'd give him an ultimatum. You or her.

Mer, I can't do that.

Suit yourself. Listen, I have to go. We're getting ready to head into the hot tub. Keep me posted on how things go and just remember...you get to determine how people treat you. Love you. Xx.

I shook my head, placing the phone face down on the counter. She made things seem so simple, but in reality—my reality—they stayed far from it.

CHAPTER TWENTY-ONE

LOREN

When we got home that night, the house was lit up—the whole bottom floor bright with lights. To my surprise, Jack's sedan was in the driveway. It was rare that he arrived home before me.

I pulled Rynlee from her car seat and headed into the house, surprised to smell cinnamon when I hit the door. As I pushed the front door open and stepped inside, the warmth of the house hitting me quickly, I gasped.

"What's going on?"

Jack was standing in the foyer. He spun to see me, a warm expression on his face. "Welcome home," he said, holding his arms out for me. I leaned in for a cautious hug.

"What are you doing? What's that smell?"

He shook his head, his smile growing as he jerked his head in the direction of the kitchen. "It's not me."

"What?"

Before he could say any more, I heard footsteps coming our direction—the unmistakable sound of her heels clicking across our hardwood floors. I braced myself, my stomach literally clenching at the thought of seeing her.

"Hello!" she said, smiling and waving as if she were a candidate in a beauty pageant.

"Hi, what, uh, what's going on?"

"Well," she stepped down off the tiny step from the kitchen into the foyer, "Jack and I spoke this morning and he mentioned how upset you've been with me." My eyes darted to Jack in a scowl.

"It's just been a difficult—"

"I know," she cut me off. "I know I haven't made any of this easy on you, but I want to fix that, Loren. I don't want you to resent me. Two separate families, all these separate lives under one roof…it puts a lot of strain on a person. I get it. You're trying to adjust to having my son here, and now I'm here too, and I'm an old woman set in my ways, not used to having a child around who I have to be careful with. All I'm saying is, I know my stay here has been difficult. I've been suffering, grieving, lost in my own world…but that doesn't excuse my behavior. So, I've spent the day cleaning the house for you—" I felt the dig in her words, though I knew Jack wouldn't hear them. *I'm not a good enough housekeeper,* she was saying. "And I've prepared meatloaf, mashed potatoes, and corn casserole. Jack said it's your favorite. Along with an apple pie." She smiled, obviously proud of herself. "I know it's not enough to totally earn your forgiveness, but I'm hoping it's a start."

Again, I noticed what I often noticed with Coralee's *apologies,* there was no semblance of the words 'I'm sorry' anywhere in them.

"Thank you, Coralee," I said after a moment because they were all waiting on a response. "That was very kind of you."

We walked into the dining room after I'd stopped by the kitchen to wash my hands, and I saw that Coralee had, in fact, prepared all of my favorite foods—coordinated by Jack, I was sure—and they were sitting out, ready to be served.

I tried not to show how impressed or hungry I was as I filled Rynlee's plate, then my own. When I sat down, Coralee began to make Jack's and then her own. As she put the last helping of Jack's food on his plate, her eyes met mine, but I refused to give her the satisfaction. I looked away instantly, sticking my fork into the food.

Before I could take the first bite, a terrifying thought filled my mind.

What if she'd poisoned us? What if this was a trap?

I looked at Rynlee, who was staring at her food without eating either and, though I knew it wasn't likely, I couldn't help wondering if she was thinking the same thing.

"Well, go on then," Jack said, reaching out for my hand. "Eat up. Mom's an excellent cook."

I paused, trying to move my way through the maze of a situation. "Well, I think I'd like to have a drink first. Rynlee, would you like some milk before you eat?" She nodded. I stood, grabbing the empty glasses in front of us. "But you guys go ahead and dig in." I knew it hadn't come across as casually as I'd hoped, but I had no choice. When Rynlee moved to take a bite, I nearly lunged at her. "Wait!" I cried, and her fork clattered back to the plate, her expression startled. "Wait, Ryn. You need to drink something first..." I looked at Jack and Coralee, who could see right through my lies.

"Oh, for goodness sake," Coralee said, shoving her fork into the food on my plate and taking a bite to prove it wasn't poisoned. "Do you honestly think I'm trying to kill you? I'm feeding my son this food." She scoffed, her jaw hung open in disbelief as she shook her head.

"I'm sorry, of course I didn't—"

"I don't think I'm hungry," she said, cutting me off and standing from the table. "Jack, would you mind cleaning all of this up?"

"Of course, Mom," he said, his eyes following her as she left the room. "Do you want some in your room?" His voice carried down the hall, but we never heard her answer. When she was far enough away Jack must've assumed she couldn't hear us, and he lifted his fork and took a bite of his food, not meeting my eyes.

"Jack, I'm sor—"

"Let's just eat, Loren. I don't want to—" He sighed. "I can't do this right now."

"I didn't think—"

"We both know what you thought. I can't do this right now."

"You have to understand where I'm coming from. My first priority isn't to protect your feelings, or even your mother's, it's to protect my child. If I thought even for a minute that she might've done something to the food and hadn't spoken up, I would've never forgiven myself. What about the peanut butter incident? Can you really blame me after all that's happened?"

He took a bite of his food, his jaw tight. "Well, I'm eating it and not dying, so I think you're fine."

"Jack, please—"

"Can we just drop it? I begged Mom to cook for us. Talked to her all day about how stressful things have been for you. I keep having her apologize; over and over she makes these statements about how sorry she is for things she didn't mean to do. Yes, I know she's made things difficult. Yes, I know the room situation is ridiculous, and I've told her as much. I go to bat for you with her all the time, just like I do for her with you. You're my wife, but she's my mom. I can't choose one over the other. Don't ask me to do that, okay? I'm trying to stay on both of your sides and keep everyone happy, but...I just can't win here."

"What's wrong? Why can't we eat?" Rynlee asked, running her fork over her food nervously.

"You can eat, sweet girl, it's fine. I'm sorry I scared you." I made my way to the kitchen and filled her glass with milk, mine with chardonnay. When I came back, they were eating in silence, and I felt about two inches tall. I handed her milk to her, sitting down in my chair.

"I'm sorry," I whispered, lifting my fork and taking a bite for good measure, though my stomach was rumbling with stress and I knew I likely wouldn't clear my plate.

"I know," he said, meeting my eyes for just a moment. "I know."

WHEN I ENTERED our bedroom that evening, Jack was waiting for me. I knew he would be, which is why I'd spent extra time with Rynlee, even once she had reluctantly gone to sleep. I wanted to avoid the conversation I knew was coming.

"Sit down, Loren," he commanded, his tone one I'd never heard from him. I saw the disappointment in his eyes, knew what I was doing to us.

I sat obediently on the edge of the bench to my vanity. "Look, Jack, I—"

"Please, just...let me talk, okay?"

I nodded, my chest tight with apprehension. There was so much I wanted to say to him, to explain, but I knew the harder I pushed to make my actions and my thoughts make sense, the more I'd push him away. My issues, the real issues weren't with Jack. I knew the situation must be tough for him. My issues were with Coralee. Our relationship had been strong before her. He'd made me laugh, made me feel secure, made me feel wanted. I'd never been looked at the way he looked at me. I wanted to show my daughter that love doesn't come easy, marriage doesn't. I wanted her to see that it was work, but that the work was worth it.

"I don't know what's happening," he said, and I bit down on my tongue to keep myself from cutting in right then. "But I know that it's not healthy. For any of us. I know that it's been a change...having us here. Me, first, and now Mom. I can't imagine what an adjustment it's been, and I'm so grateful for your kindness toward us."

Suddenly, I felt like I was getting broken up with. My chest was tight, ready to explode with tears. I couldn't let him end this. I couldn't let him walk away. I couldn't lose anyone else.

"I think we both know this isn't working. I just..." He rubbed his hands over the thighs of his plaid pajama pants, staring at the wall in front of him. "I don't know what to do." He looked at me then. "I love you so much."

"I love you, too," I said, breaking my rule about speaking before I knew he was done.

"But I love my mom, too. She's all—I'm all she has left, and she was all I had for a very long time. When my dad got sick, it was just us, dealing with it all. I know you can't understand it. I know you must think I'm crazy, but she's always been good to me. She's always taken care of me. She's my mom, Lor, and she's really hurting right now. But keeping her here is hurting you, so what am I supposed to do? I just feel so lost and overwhelmed." His voice broke and he stopped speaking, but I could see the figurative weight I'd placed on his shoulders without realizing it. I'd been so focused on my own issues with Coralee, I hadn't thought of what this must be doing to him.

"I'm sorry, Jack. I've been so foolish."

"You haven't—"

"No, no, I have." I leaned off the bench, lowering myself to the carpet on my knees and moving across to him. When I reached his legs, I took hold of his hands, staring into his eyes. "You're right, this isn't easy for any of us, but I could've made it better. I think the initial impression with your mother being here—the allergy incident—it's just soured me to her and maybe I've placed unnecessary blame on her, but I just get worried about Rynlee and that's all I can think about. She's been the source of a lot of stress where my daughter's concerned. You see that, don't you?" He nodded, but didn't say anything. "Maybe I jumped to conclusions on some of it. Maybe I was too harsh. If that's the case, I'm really, really sorry. I love you so much." I squeezed his hands. "I'm so glad you're in my life. Family means sacrifice, and if this is a sacrifice I have to make for a while longer, I will. Whatever it takes to keep our family together." I kissed his fingers, looking back up to see his eyes locked on mine.

When he smiled, my heart warmed instantly. He leaned down, his lips on mine, and the feeling was so foreign I felt fresh tears prick my eyes. Aside from a peck on the lips as he was walking out the door most mornings, we'd hardly had time to speak in private, let alone kiss like we were now, *let alone* all the things I'd been dying to do with a moment to ourselves...

I stood from the ground, refusing to remove my lips from his, and wrapped my arms around his neck, moaning under my breath. He responded to the sound, pulling me onto his lap and leaning back onto the bed. I kissed his lips, his cheek, his jaw, his neck, growing more impatient with every move.

His hands moved to lift my shirt, and I saw the fire in his eyes that I felt in my belly as I sat up tearing the shirt from my body in one swift motion.

He looked me over, his eyes growing wider as he sat up, his kisses covering my chest, my skin burning every place he touched. I wanted him. I wanted him more than I'd ever wanted anything in my life. At that moment, nothing else mattered.

Knock, knock.

And just like that, the moment ended. I shoved back away from him, reaching for my shirt as he rolled me over, standing from the bed in an instant.

"Just a minute," I called, pulling the shirt over my head and praying Rynlee wouldn't open the door just yet. Had I thought to lock it? Of course not.

Before my shirt was completely covering my midriff, the door sprang open, and I was surprised to see Coralee standing in our doorway. Her makeup had been removed, her long, silver hair hung down around her shoulders, wet from a recent shower it seemed. It was the first time I'd seen her looking less than perfect.

"Mom?" Jack asked, clearing his throat. "What is it? What's the matter?"

I watched him shift in place, shoving his legs from one

side to the other to hide the physical proof of what we'd been doing.

She looked at him with wide eyes and then, without a moment's notice, she burst into tears.

I moved toward her instinctually, but Jack was there first, his arms around her. "What is it?" he asked again. "What happened?"

She let out a loud sob, her shoulders shaking. "I thought I could handle it. I thought if I kept myself busy today I could —but I can't. I can't do this anymore. I'm not strong enough."

"What are you talking about?" he asked, his tone soft as he cradled his mother in his arms, patting her wet hair. Jack was a nurturer. I supposed I'd known that after our first encounter when he'd bandaged me up, but watching it happen made my heart swell with pride. I'd always heard that you should find a man who treats his mother well, because that's how you'll be treated, too. And I did want to be treated this way—cherished, protected. Loved. I wanted to be loved. If Jack's affection toward his mother was a sign of what I could expect for the rest of my life, I wanted to hold onto that with both hands.

I moved forward, placing a cautious hand on Jack's back to let him—them—know I was there.

"Today's our...anniversary," she cried, sniffling loudly before she looked up to meet his eyes, then mine.

"Your anniversary is in August," he said, his brow furrowed.

"Not our wedding anniversary," she explained through her tears. "Today's the day we met, the day of our very first date." She stood up, wiping tears from her eyes.

"I'm so sorry, Coralee," I said, trying to offer comfort, though I felt I wasn't welcome.

To my surprise, the smile she offered seemed genuine. "Thank you. I'm sorry to come down here like this." She was looking back at Jack then. "I usually feel okay, but today has been..."

"Hard," Jack finished for her.

"Of course it has," I added. "That's totally understandable."

She didn't look at me that time, but nodded slightly to acknowledge the comment. "I hate to ask this," she said, playing with the sleeve of her robe. "It's stupid, forget it." She turned to walk away abruptly, but Jack stopped her.

"What is it? Anything you need."

"Would you...Jack, would you come to my room and stay with me tonight? Just until I fall asleep. I think maybe talking with someone, a bit of a distraction, would help." She paused as he looked at me, then added, "You can say no."

I froze, waiting to see what his answer was going to be. No matter what, I knew I couldn't insert my opinion here, even if my opinion was that this was the most absurd request I'd ever heard. Instead, I waited, my eyes unblinking as I watched him survey my face.

Finally, he turned back to his mother and sighed. "Of course. Maybe I can make us some tea, that always makes you feel better."

I felt my chest swell with hurt and confusion, my jaw locked tight. It was ridiculous. What an absolutely insane request. She was a grown woman. He'd been put off by Rynlee's night terrors but his mother's, *sure, that was fine.* I ran my tongue over my teeth, trying to calm myself down. I needed to find the resolve I'd been gripping so tightly to. She beamed at him, clasping her hands together in front of her chest. "Oh, Jack, what did I do to deserve a son like you? You always know what to do to make Momma feel better." She patted his arm, then looked at me. "Is this okay, Loren? Can I borrow your husband for the night? You won't miss him too much, will you?"

I chewed the inside of my lip as the forced smile filled my face. "Not at all."

Her lips curled into a grin, her eyes cold and unmoving. Jack kissed my cheek, though I didn't return the affection. He whispered that he'd see me later, and ushered her out into the hall. When his eyes met mine, I looked away, letting him know how angry I felt. He shut the door, though, apparently not caring.

In the battle of me and Coralee, he'd chosen her.

She'd won. We both knew it.

But the game wasn't over.

It was just beginning.

CHAPTER TWENTY-TWO

LOREN

The following night when someone knocked on our bedroom door, I groaned in anticipation of seeing Coralee's face again. Jack and I hadn't spoken about his mother's behavior the night before, and I felt I was in no position to bring it up unless he did, but I couldn't let it become a habit.

Jack was standing on the far side of the room, searching for the pajama pants he'd discarded when he'd gotten dressed that morning. "Just a minute," he called, frantically pulling his pants from a drawer and pulling them over his legs.

I stepped up to the door, my hand shaking with dread.

I stared into the space where Coralee's face should've been, then looked down with a gasp. "Ryn, what is it?"

She twisted her foot in the carpet underneath her. "Could I sleep in here again?"

"What's wrong?" Jack asked, standing next to me now. He lowered himself so he was eye level to her and held out his hands. To my relief, she leaned into them, pressing her cheek into his shoulder.

"I just want to sleep in here."

"Did something happen?" I asked, bending down next to them as well.

"My door keeps opening," she said.

My blood ran cold at her words, though I tried to hide the fear from my expression. "What do you mean your door keeps opening?"

"It won't stay shut."

Jack sighed, glancing at me with a look that said I shouldn't get any hairbrained ideas. "Let's go check it out, okay?" He scooped Rynlee up, and together we headed down the hall and toward her bedroom. The door was open, and Jack pulled it closed.

We waited.

After a few moments, he twisted the knob and pushed it open, staring around the dark room. I reached beside him, running my hand along the wall until I felt the light switch. I flipped it on and followed Jack and Rynlee inside.

Once we were in, Jack set Rynlee down, studying the latch. He ran his finger over it, watching the black metal piece slide in and out with ease. Afterward, he shut the door, moving around it to check the frame and hinges. When he was done, he stood back up. "Everything looks okay, Ryn. Maybe you just weren't getting the door latched all the way." His tone was patronizing and she nodded without argument, but the argument was present in my mind. She'd never had trouble latching her door before, and she'd lived in the room her whole life.

Choosing my words carefully, I bent down next to her

and wrapped my arms around her waist. "When did the door open, baby? When you first shut it?"

She shook her head.

"When then?"

"When I woke up in the night," she said quietly. I hated what Jack's skepticism had done to my normally confident child. I looked up at him, waiting for him to explain it away.

Right on cue, he said, "It was probably just the heat kicking on, the shift in air pressure can do that, especially in older houses."

I wrapped my arms around her tighter. I didn't want to argue, especially not in front of Rynlee; she was dealing with enough. Still, I didn't need him to tell me what was normal in an older house, particularly not *this* house. This was the house I'd grown up in, lived in my whole life—barring a few years of college—and raised my family in. I knew what was normal for it. Doors opening just because, wasn't normal.

Instead of throwing out all of the valid points I had to disprove his theory, I nodded and took my daughter's hand as I stood. "Okay. Well, tonight you can sleep with us again if you don't want to stay in here."

Her smile was small, but it was there. Jack nodded, his lips a tight line, but didn't disagree. I knew he thought I was coddling her, rather than facing the issues head on—*pot meet kettle*—but I couldn't help it. I believed Rynlee when she said something wasn't right, and I was going to do everything in my power to prove it to Jack, too.

"Hey, do you think you could take her up? I'm going to run downstairs and get a drink of water."

He nodded. "Sure."

When they headed down the hall, I pulled the door shut behind us and walked down the stairs toward the kitchen.

When I made it to the kitchen, guided by the light above the stove until I reached the light switch, I turned toward the dining room rather than the sink.

I hated to lie to Jack, even about something as small as this, but I was running out of options. I moved to the rounded window seat under the bay window in our dining room and lifted the seat, digging through old cords and batteries. Finally, I spotted what I was looking for—a flash of white near the bottom of the chest.

I pulled the two pieces of the baby monitor out, dusting off the screen and the camera's lens. It had been about a year since the camera had adorned Rynlee's wall, but I was sure the nail was still there...waiting.

I hoped Jack wouldn't notice it, and I would explain it to Rynlee as soon as she did, but I hoped I could slide it back into place in her bedroom without disrupting anything.

I flipped off the light and hurried back up the stairs, hoping my semi-formed plan would work. I opened Rynlee's door and stepped inside, but stopped and sucked in a breath.

The light to the tiny bedroom was on.

I stared around, the hair on my arms standing up with fear as I waited for something to happen. The room smelled...musty, mixed with sage and lavender. It smelled like Coralee. I was sure I hadn't noticed the smell before.

I inhaled, furrowing my brow. None of it made any sense. I hadn't been gone long enough for such an unfamiliar smell to have filled the air, yet it had.

I shook my head to clear a voice that sounded strangely like Jack's reminding me that it was probably just the smell of our heat kicking on, and walked across the room to where her shelf of stuffed animals hung. Rather than hanging the camera on the wall, where it would likely be noticed, I placed it in between a few of her toys, running the wire down along her bookshelf and plugging it in behind her mini-recliner.

I glanced over my shoulder, the silence in the room deafening to my extra-sensitive ears. Every pop of the floor or creak of the walls caused me to jump. When I stood, I looked over my handiwork carefully. If they weren't looking for it, I hoped they wouldn't see it. Then, before I went to my bedroom, I turned on the monitor in my hands, looking at myself on the screen. It was a strange feeling, seeing myself there on the tiny, black and white screen, my back to the camera. I glanced over my shoulder, staring at the camera. It all felt surreal, but for the first time in a long time, I had a glimmer of hope as I stared into the screen. The woman there was strong, she'd survived the worst of the worst, and she'd survive this.

No matter what, I had to survive this.

CHAPTER TWENTY-THREE

LOREN

I couldn't sleep.

Not that that was at all unusual lately.

I sat in the oversized chair near the window of our bedroom with my feet curled up under me, a glass of moscato in one hand, a paperback I'd been meaning to read in the other. The monitor was balanced in my lap and every twenty minutes, the screen would go dark until I pushed the button to wake it up.

Try as I might, I couldn't bring myself to get into the story in my head, because I felt the imminent nightmare that had become my life growing more and more real. What was I going to do if I couldn't convince Jack I wasn't insane? What was I going to do if I *truly was*?

I gave up, setting the book down on my lap and taking another sip of wine. I took a breath, running my hands over my face and sighing. I was stuck in a perpetual place of fear and confusion, and it all pointed back to the moment Coralee entered my life. But honestly, I wasn't sure I could blame her for *all* of it. I wasn't sure I couldn't either, but I just...*didn't know.* I didn't do well with not knowing, truth be told. Especially not when it involved Rynlee. She was too important to just hang on by a thread, and that was exactly what I felt like I was doing.

A yawn escaped my throat, reminding me just how little sleep I'd had in the last few days, but as much as I wanted to lie down, close my eyes, and let sleep take me, I couldn't.

I opened my eyes and lifted the monitor from my lap, tapping the top of the device to reawaken the screen. When the image came to life, I dropped the monitor instantly, my hands shaking, and pushed myself away from it as if the person I was staring at could come through the screen.

Coralee stood in the center of Rynlee's room, her head turning this way and that as she surveyed the dark space. Her movements were slow and methodical, as though she believed there was no chance she could be caught as she began to pace. She leaned against the far wall, her forehead pressed to it.

What is she doing?

I scooted forward on the chair again, picking up the monitor slowly, as if any movement might disturb her. But it wouldn't. I had the perfect opportunity to catch her doing whatever it was she had planned.

Part of me considered waking Jack up, but I knew if we interrupted her too early, there was a chance she could explain it all away. I stood, keeping my eyes on the screen as I made my way toward my nightstand, trading out the glass of wine for my phone. I turned on the camera, switching it to video mode and hitting the red button that would record my proof.

I held the phone above the monitor as Coralee made one final round from one side of the room to the next before she disappeared to the right of the camera, where I could no longer see her. Had she seen the camera? I watched the screen closely, listening even closer. My heart thudded in my chest, my breathing shallow as I waited for her to pull the camera down, so I was staring directly into her eyes, or to hear her footsteps headed down the hall, demanding to know what I'd been doing spying on her, but it didn't happen. The screen was blank and the room was silent.

When it felt like my heart could take no more stress, I moved toward the bed, cutting off the video recording and setting the monitor on Jack's bedside table.

"Jack," I whispered, shaking him. "Jack, wake up."

He stirred, rubbing his cheek against the pillow in a half-asleep state before his eyes fluttered open. When he saw my face, he shot up, letting out a yelp. "Jesus, Loren, what the hell are you doing?"

"Something's wrong," I said.

"What do you mean? What happened?" His voice filled with fear as he pulled the covers from his legs and pushed himself up in bed, his gaze searching the room for a threat.

"It's...it's your mother. She's the one who's been in Rynlee's room."

His eyes flickered distrust—I didn't miss it—but he didn't dismiss my concern. "What do you mean?"

"I...well, I turned on her baby monitor in her room. Just in case, you know? And...she's in there right now."

I pointed to the monitor and Jack lowered his gaze to it, lifting it to his face. He was silent for a moment. "I...I don't see anything, Loren. What do *you* see?" He held it out so I could look at the screen, though Coralee still wasn't in view.

"Nothing, of course. Not right now. She's off screen somewhere. But she was there, pacing around."

"Are you sure you're not just tired?"

"*I'm not!*" I insisted, trying to reign in my frustration. "I have her on my phone. Look." I opened up my gallery, clicking on the video and turning it over to him. He stared at the screen, his expression transitioning from denial to confusion within seconds.

"What is she doing?"

"I don't know, but you believe me now, don't you? That she's up to something?"

"Up to something?" He scowled. "Easy, Nancy Drew. Let's just go down there and see what she's doing. I'm sure there's an explanation."

"What explanation could she have for being in Rynlee's room in the middle of the night?"

He shook his head, not offering an answer, but stood up and made his way across the room. I followed close behind.

We made our way down the hall and into Rynlee's bedroom, stepping into the dark and quiet room with gusto.

"Mom?" Jack called, ending our futile search. The room was empty. I moved around quickly, looking for Coralee. I lifted the edge of the comforter. "Well, I don't think she's going to be under there," he said, giving me a playful eye roll.

I stepped into the closet, my chest heaving with heavy breaths. Two totes sat beside the built-in bookcase, and all of her clothes were shoved to one side again, but there was no sign of my mother-in-law.

"Where is she?" I asked, spinning round in circles with my arms to my sides, the frantic fear swelling in my chest must've been evident on my face because Jack took a step toward me, placing a careful hand on my shoulder.

"She probably went back upstairs to bed."

"We never saw her leave...I never saw her leave," I said, staring down at the monitor in my hand.

"It's possible she left when we were talking. You didn't have your eyes on it the whole time."

"I never looked away," I told him, though I knew it wasn't completely true. There may have been a second or two when I couldn't have been watching.

"Let's just go back to bed. We can talk to her in the morning." He pulled my arm gently.

"No," I said, a bit too loudly. "No. I need to see her tonight." Panic set in. I stormed past him, hurrying up the stairs before he could stop me. My eyes burned with fresh tears as I rushed down the hall, my footsteps giving her warning that I was coming, but I didn't care.

I thought for a split second about knocking, but decided against it, reaching my hand out for the knob and launching myself forward.

THUD.

I slammed into the door, the knob locked firmly into position as I ricocheted off the wood and backward. Jack was right behind me, taking hold of my shoulders. "Are you okay?" he asked, leaning down to examine me, though we both knew he couldn't see much in the dark.

Just then, the door opened and Coralee stood in front of us, her eyes traveling up and down my body once. "What was that?"

"Why was your door locked?" I demanded.

"Perhaps because *you* seem to have an aversion to knocking." She crossed her arms over her chest.

"Mom," Jack interrupted us, cutting off the argument before it could begin. "Were you just in Rynlee's room?"

She cocked her head to the side, and I sucked in a deep

breath, feeling the anger swell in my chest. "When do you mean?"

"Just a few minutes ago," I told her, just daring her to lie. If she lied, I'd have all the proof I needed that I'd been right. Finally, Jack would believe me—

"Oh, yes, I was. Sorry, did I disturb you?" Her eyes were wide with fake remorse.

"What were you doing in there?" I demanded. "Why were you in her room in the middle of the night?"

Coralee looked at me, then at Jack. "Well, I wasn't going to say anything, but I think your daughter's been in my room."

"What do you mean?" Jack asked. "Why would you think that?"

She pressed her lips together, letting out a quiet 'hmph.' "Well, my favorite necklace has been missing for days. I caught the girl playing with it the other day up here and asked her to leave it alone. But it's gone missing and, well, I assumed she took it."

"Rynlee wouldn't have done that," Jack said. "She's very well behaved. She wouldn't have taken anything." I looked up at him, surprised to hear him taking my side for once.

"Well, I'm not sure what to think, then. Unless you have ghosts, Rynlee seems the most likely culprit," Coralee said.

"Like Jack said, she wouldn't have taken it. She knows better than that. She doesn't steal, and she'd have no use for your necklace. When did you find her up here?"

"A day or so ago," she said, waving her hand in the air as if it didn't matter. "I didn't think anything of it at the time."

"She was in your bedroom?" I asked. Rynlee had never been one to travel to the other levels of our house, unless I was there with her, but lately, she didn't even like to be out of the room I was in, so her accusation was especially ridiculous.

"Yes, going through my jewelry case. It would've been a harmless game of dress up for her, except most of my jewelry is very expensive."

"Why didn't you mention it to me?" I asked.

"Or me?" Jack added. "If she was caught in here, we would've wanted to address it right then." He placed a comforting hand on my back.

"Well, Loren doesn't take kindly to the things I say, so I assumed it was a situation I could handle on my own."

"I don't *take kindly to*—"

"*Mom, enough,*" Jack cut in, sounding exasperated. "Did you find the necklace in Rynlee's room or not?"

"No, I did not," she said, her nose in the air. "It's around here somewhere. Anyway, how did the two of you know I was in her room? She wasn't in there."

"She's not in her room because something's been scaring her at night," I said. "Is that you?"

She dropped her jaw dramatically. "Of course not. I stopped rocking in my chair at night. I've made sure to keep quiet after she goes to bed so I wouldn't disturb her."

"She said someone's been opening her door."

"She said her door's been opening," Jack corrected. "Not that someone's been opening it."

"But how did you know Rynlee was gone if you haven't been going down there checking?"

Coralee opened her mouth, then closed it again, and I saw a hint of defeat in her eyes. When she spoke again, I thought I'd won. "I heard her footsteps headed down the hall."

"Why would you look for it in the middle of the night? Why not just come ask me?"

"I didn't want her to get into trouble," she said, her answer already prepared for that one. "And I couldn't sleep knowing it was gone. It was a present from Malcolm."

I nodded, my anger overflowing. I couldn't hold it in anymore. Her indifference to the torment she was inflicting on my family had driven me mad. I tried to channel my inner-Meredith for the sake of my daughter if nothing else, my blood boiling as I stared at her. "Do you enjoy this? You're scaring her, Coralee! You're scaring a five-year-old. Is that what you want?"

"Of course not—" she said.

"Loren—" Jack said at the same time. I looked up at him. "Look, we're all just tired, okay? We'll talk to Rynlee about the necklace in the morning and figure out what's going on. For now, I have an early morning. Can we all just agree to go to bed?"

I tasted blood suddenly and released the inside of my lip from in between my teeth. Helplessness was not an emotion I carried well, but I'd felt nothing more strongly than that from the moment Coralee entered my home. "I want her out," I said. "I want her out tonight."

"You can't kick her out in the middle of the night," Jack argued.

"You can't kick me out at all," Coralee said, her voice filling the room. I spun to look at her.

I was done holding my tongue, done sitting quietly while she wreaked havoc on my life. I couldn't do it anymore. I could feel the blood pooling in my palms as I clenched my fists and my nails broke the skin. Enough was enough. "Excuse me? This is my house. You've done nothing but make my daughter and me completely uncomfortable from the moment you stepped across that threshold. I can and will make you leave whenever I choose," I looked at Jack, "so, I guess you have a decision to make. If you can't back me up, I'm sorry, Jack, but you'll have to go, too."

He jerked his head back, just as surprised by my words as I was. "You don't mean that."

"I don't want you to leave, but I can't live like this. I can't ask my daughter to live like this."

"I'm not leaving," Coralee said, her voice firm. "Would you really ask my son to choose between us? His *only* family?"

"If you leave, he won't have to make that choice. But then, I think that's what you've wanted all along." I said the words before I'd thought them through, but once they were out, I realized I believed they were true. Getting Jack and me apart could well have been her endgame all along.

She pursed her lips, but didn't say anything right away. When she did speak, her voice was soft. "You know nothing about me. How dare you presume to know what I want?"

"I know enough," I said. "What is it? Am I not good enough for your son? Is that your plan? Run me off? Are you really petty enough to frighten a child to get that? She's just a baby, Coralee! She's innocent in all of this."

"You've labeled me a villain from the moment we met—"

"That's not true! I wanted to get to know you. I wanted to feel like a family with you. I haven't had that in so long..." My voice cracked suddenly. "Rynlee never got to know her grandparents. You were her only chance. I wanted this to work, Coralee, but you've made it abundantly clear that you don't want the same thing."

She folded her arms over her chest and glanced at the floor, nodding. "Well, I'm sorry if that's what you think of me, Loren. But despite your putrid view of me, I wanted this to work as well. The only thing that's ever mattered to me," she reached out and touched Jack's arm, "is that my son is happy. And I thought you made him happy. But since you two've been married, all you do is fight and argue. Apparently, you can't even make time to be together as husband and wife because your daughter is always in bed with you—"

"What?" I demanded, looking at Jack, venom pulsing through my veins. "Seriously?"

His face began to grow pink. "Mom, that's enough."

"We are unhappy because we've allowed this dark cloud into our marriage." I stepped toward her. "*You* are that dark cloud, Coralee. You are. And our sex life is certainly none of your business, but if you must know, you've been more of a distraction that Rynlee would ever be. She would've never been in our bed if you hadn't been trying to scare her all this time."

"Loren!" Jack yelled, his voice echoing through the house so much that I jumped. We both turned to look at him. "Both of you—I said that's enough." Before he could say anything else, I heard Rynlee's cry from downstairs. We had woken her up.

I sighed. "I'm going to go take care of her." I pointed at Coralee. "I mean it, Jack. This is the last night of this. I want her out."

I didn't bother looking at Coralee as I walked out of the bedroom and toward the stairs. I didn't feel relief like I'd expected. I supposed I wouldn't feel that until she disappeared from my house for good. But I'd finally said what I needed to—it was all laid out there, and Jack could do what he wanted to with it.

Either way, I was closer than ever to getting rid of Coralee, and that was all that mattered to me anymore.

CHAPTER TWENTY-FOUR

LOREN

The next morning, when I woke, my head was heavy with sleep. Unlike most nights lately, I hadn't had a nightmare and I hadn't woken up multiple times. I'd slept soundly. I supposed going so long without sleep had finally caught up with me.

I shot up in bed, looking around the room for my missing husband. Beside me, Rynlee stirred. Her eyes opened, tiny fists moving to rub them.

"Momma?"

I smoothed her messy hair. "It's okay, baby. I didn't mean to wake you up."

Her mouth was already forming an 'O' as she gave in to a yawn. Within seconds, her head fell back on her pillow and her breathing had grown regular again. I slid from the bed carefully, freezing each time she stirred.

I tiptoed across the room, headed for the door, and then down the hallway. I could hear quiet voices on the floor below. Coralee hadn't left, after all. I can't lie and say I totally expected her to, but I couldn't believe Jack hadn't backed me up at all.

When I made it to the first floor, the talking ceased, and I heard footsteps headed my way. Jack stepped into the living room, his expression wary.

"Hey," he said, waiting for me to make a move.

I was stony, my lips a thin line as I addressed him. "Good morning. What's going on?"

"Mom wants to talk to you."

"I have nothing to say to her, Jack," I said. I was done with the half-attempts at making amends when things had gone too far.

"Just-just...hear her out. Please, for me?" His eyes were hopeful, his hands clasped together as if he were praying. "If you'll just hear what she has to say, and then if you still want her out, I promise I'll make it happen."

Those words and those words alone were what made me agree. I nodded slightly, knowing nothing could make me change my mind. "Fine."

At my words, her heels clicked across the hardwood, and I looked over, watching her enter the room. She wore the silver dress she'd been wearing the day I met her, and her long, gray hair was tied up in a bun. She smiled at me, an expression that looked so foreign on her face I had to do a double take.

"Loren," she said, clearing her throat. She looked to Jack, who nodded encouragingly, before looking down at the floor to continue. "I, well, I'm sorry." She paused, finally looking up. Her eyes weren't the stone I was used to, instead there was warmth there I'd never seen from her. "I'm sorry for any distress I've caused you and your family. I'm sorry for disrupting your home and your lives. I hadn't realized how much I've done to upset you until I spoke with Jack last night. He…he put things into perspective for me about how you feel, and I want you to know, it was never my intention to do this."

I watched her mouth move, heard the words coming out, but I couldn't feel what she was saying. It seemed like a dream, a script she'd been given. I'd heard it too many times from her. I wouldn't change my mind. It was too late. "Thank you, Coralee."

"And…I found the wallpaper. For the room upstairs. Jack said it came from a small boutique, that it was custom. I found one online that I'm sure is it. I've ordered it, and I'm having it reinstalled Wednesday. It was the earliest they could come. I'm terribly embarrassed by my actions. I had a yellow bedroom when I was a little girl, and then Malcolm painted our bedroom yellow after we bought our first home. I think…I think I just needed to feel at home again, but it wasn't fair to you. I haven't been in my right mind since Malcolm's passing, and I'm truly sorry for the way I've behaved." Her eyes grew wide and she reached behind her. "I have something for you. Both of you. As a way to make amends." She held her hand out, a paper in it. I leaned forward, noticing the small picture of a cabin in the top, left hand corner.

Romantic Cabin Getaway, the headline read. I skimmed the small paragraph below it, reading about a hot tub and relaxing scenery all just a few miles from the city.

I glanced up at her. "What's this?"

"I've booked you a cabin," she cleared her throat, "you and Jack. And while you're gone, I'll have the wallpaper installed and an air purifier hooked up in my room to get rid of the smell. I've also got a very good tailor to come by and look at that quilt of your grandmother's. I'll work on getting out the stain, and she'll repair the fabric. It won't be as good as before, but we'll make it so you have to look hard to see where the damage is." She ran her finger across her palm. "I-I know I can't fix everything I've done wrong, but I will do what I can to make this right." I watched her glance back down at the floor, waiting for me to speak.

"Thank you, Coralee. This is very kind of you, but...we really can't accept it."

"Nonsense, of course you can. It's a paid-for week away, no stress. And when you come home, your house will be returned to the way you had it."

"Coralee, I can't let you pay for this. You should be saving your money for when you're back on your own. Besides, I can't leave Rynlee alone. And I have the store to take care of." I didn't know her financial situation, but from the looks of the cabin, it hadn't come cheap.

She waved off my concerns. "Oh, don't worry about that. I've been living here all this time and you haven't asked me to pitch in with rent or utilities or even food. I've only paid for a few meals since I've been here, and you hardly ate them. It's the least I can do. And I'm happy to watch Rynlee for you. And I can run whatever errands you need me to for the store. You deserve some time off. You can't do everything without a break. You both need some time off together."

I glanced at Jack. It was preposterous. If there had ever been a time when I shouldn't have been allowed a day—let alone a week—off, *this* was that time.

"I just, I'm not sure I can swing it right now."

"What is there to *swing?*" she asked, her eyes blinking rapidly. "I've taken care of everything."

Jack spoke up. "Lor, I really think we need this right now.

We could never have done it for ourselves. We'd always find an excuse not to between Rynlee, life, and two businesses to run, but…it's already done. We can at least enjoy it, right?" His smile was sad and unconvinced. He didn't believe I would take it, but he needed me to.

I popped my neck, bouncing my head side to side as I thought. "I'll have to try to get ahold of Meredith. I need to see if she can come back for the week. If not, I just don't see how we could make it work. Becky can't open and close with no lunch all week. It's not fair."

"I'm perfectly capable of giving your employee lunch," Coralee said.

I disregarded her comment entirely. If she wasn't capable of remembering basic things, why on earth would I trust her to learn and run my store in such a short amount of time? "And…as far as Rynlee, I think I'd feel more comfortable with Sarah keeping her. Or Meredith if she will come home. She's just…she knows them, you know? They've taken care of her her whole life." I said the words softly, awaiting the argument that would surely ensue.

To my surprise, Coralee's lips formed a small, tight smile, her eyes unwavering. "Whatever you think is best."

Jack looked at her and then to me, hope filling his face. He saw this as a new start, I knew. He thought things were good now, but I wasn't so sure. I couldn't get a read on Coralee and I didn't know what her endgame was, but I didn't believe her intentions were pure. My mother-in-law was a monster, and whether or not my husband saw it yet, her innocent act wasn't fooling me.

CHAPTER TWENTY-FIVE

LOREN

C oralee wants us to go out of town for the week. She purchased us a cabin. Any chance you could come home and help with the store for the time being? Jack and I could really use some time.

I held my breath and sent the text to Meredith as I turned the key in the lock to the store. I'd already asked Sarah to keep Rynlee if we decided to go, half-hoping she'd say she couldn't so I'd have an excuse not to go, but of course, she'd *be happy to.*

Damn my amazing friends.

Becky pulled into the lot just after me, carrying a tray of brown coffee cups—latte for her, flat white for me, and a hot chocolate for Ryn.

"Morning," I said, holding the door open for her as she hurried past me, smelling of coconut shampoo.

"Morning." She set the tray of drinks down, pulling them from their holders and passing them out. "You look like you need this," she said as she handed me mine. "Long night?"

I held the cup with two hands, wrapping my fingers

around its warm base. "You could say that." I moved to the wall and flipped on the overhead light, turning the sign around so that the 'Open' side was showing.

"You didn't have to come in so early," she said. "Opening is the easy part, you know."

I nodded. I did know. "I know. I had to get out of the house," I told her, too tired to care.

"Everything okay?" She moved behind the counter, unlocking the cash register to put the till inside and turning on the monitor.

"Mother-in-law drama," I told her. I hadn't told Becky about my issues with Coralee, and I hadn't planned to, but I desperately needed to talk to someone. And with Meredith gone, Becky was one of the only women left in my life who I trusted.

"Ooooh, trouble in paradise." She wiggled her eyebrows, leaning across the counter. "Give me all the dirty *deets*."

I laughed, looking over her shoulder. Rynlee had settled into her chair in my office, completely absorbed in her tablet and hot chocolate. While she was there, I lowered my voice, starting from the beginning and telling Becky everything that had gone wrong since my mother-in-law walked through my front door.

When I was finished, she had her hand over her mouth, her eyes wide. "Oh, my God, Loren. I had no idea you were going through all of that."

"You don't think I'm crazy for being so upset?" I asked, relieved to finally be taken seriously.

She shook her head. "I think you're surprisingly calm for dealing with so much."

I let out a breath of relief, leaning further onto the counter as hot tears filled my eyes.

"What is it?" she asked.

"I just…Meredith's usually who I go to with this sort of thing, and Jack thinks I'm overreacting. I hadn't said all of it out loud before, and I wasn't sure if it was all in my head. It feels really, really good to have someone to talk to."

She placed her hand on mine, her eyes incredibly too kind. Why hadn't I talked to her before? Becky had proven over and over again how much I could rely on her.

But she was leaving me, too.

Just like my parents. Just like Travis. Just like Meredith. Just like Jack would if I didn't make an effort to fix our marriage.

"I need to go to the cabin," I said with a sigh, the reality of it hitting me. "I need to get Jack alone so I can talk to him about his mother, convince him that she needs to move out."

She nodded. "Yeah, you can't go on like this, Lor. You'll lose your mind. What do you need from me?"

"Well, I'm trying to find someone to come in and help you with lunches and stuff for the week. Do you have any ideas?"

Her eyes lit up. "Actually, I was going to tell you I think I have someone in mind for you to interview for my position. A girl I went to school with, Jackie. She's super sweet, customers would love her, and she's looking for work that would be more during the day. She works at Rigley's right now, but they have her working overnight. Most of the time she's the only one there because who comes in a gas station at midnight except the odd person passing through, and it just…it makes me nervous. She interviewed at Darla's Cafe for a day shift, but I think you should snatch her up before they make her an offer. Maybe I could train her while you're gone and she could cover my lunch, but I'll bring something to eat here so I can help if I need to."

"She sounds great," I said, "but are you sure you'd be okay with that? It's asking so much of you." I chewed my lip, thinking over the possibility.

"It's not at all. I'm happy to do it. You deserve a break, and it'd make me feel better about leaving you in the middle of all of this. Besides, Jackie's great. We'll have fun."

I squeezed her hand back, already feeling the weight lifting from my shoulders. "You're the best, you know that? Can she come in this afternoon for an interview?"

"I'll text her and see," she said, lowering her voice as our first customer entered the shop. "Morning, Ms. Delores."

"Thank you," I told her. "Seriously."

She smiled. "I'm happy to help. If it means getting rid of your...*problem*...I'll do whatever I can."

BECKY and I closed up the shop together that night, going over the plans for the upcoming week. She was right, Jackie was exactly what I was looking for in a new employee. Though I would've still preferred to keep the old one, she'd fit in nicely.

Meredith still hadn't texted me back, which I was taking as a *no* to my request, but I knew I couldn't let it deter me. With Becky and Sarah to help me, we were going to make it happen. I'd go away with Jack and make him see reason.

Fix our marriage first. *Then* make him see reason.

Jackie would start the next day, she'd relieve Becky for lunch, but Becky would stick around in the building during her break to make sure things went smoothly. They'd open and close together to make sure Jackie was a pro by the time Becky left.

I made a mental note to write out a large bonus check, as large as we could afford, to Becky when I got home.

I was going to drop Rynlee off at Sarah's the next morning when we left for our trip, letting her know that Coralee was at our house and she'd be much more comfortable on her own.

She didn't argue. They were making it way too easy on me, and I was incredibly grateful to have such a support system behind me, especially since I'd never stopped to appreciate it before.

"Take care of the place, okay?" I asked, hugging Becky in the parking lot once I'd gotten Rynlee hooked in.

"Everything'll be fine here. You just relax and have some fun. Think of it as the honeymoon you never got to have."

"Something tells me it won't feel anything like that. It's got Coralee all over it."

"Hey, hate her all you want—and with good reason—but that doesn't mean you can't enjoy the spoils."

"If Meredith comes home, can you have her call me?"

She closed her eyes, nodding slowly. "When do you think she'll be back?" Her question was weighted, I knew. Both of us had experienced Meredith's whimsical betrayal before, but never for this long.

"I honestly don't know if she will," I said, shrugging one shoulder, trying to hide the pain I felt uttering those words. She *had* to come back. I couldn't go on like this much longer. "But I hope soon."

"You don't deserve this, Lor. Any of this, but especially this. You need to tell her how hard this is on us when she disappears."

"I will," I promised, though we both knew that was a lie. "As soon as I see her again."

Her brown hair whipped around her face, the wind beginning to pick up speed from the impending storm. "If you need anything, just call," she said. "But we'll hold down the fort here."

"Thank you again. For…well, for everything. Be safe going home." I waved my hand awkwardly as she backed away.

"You too."

With that, I was in the car and on my way home. I checked my phone at a stoplight, spying a missed call from Jack, but still nothing from Meredith. I groaned. Becky was right. This wasn't unlike Meredith, but that didn't make it okay. It was harder on me than ever this time, both because of the length of her disappearance but also because of everything else I was dealing with. But I'd never been one for confrontation, especially not with someone I cared about.

Meredith was the only family I'd had all my life. It was hard for me to stand up to her and rare that I needed to, but it needed to be done. When I heard from her next, whatever city or country she was in, I would let her know how I felt. I promised myself I would.

A few minutes later, Rynlee was falling asleep in her seat and we were pulling into the driveway.

I sat still, staring at her in the rearview mirror. I felt like it had been so long since we'd had a day together—just the two of us. I used to spend so much time just watching her, watching the way she chewed her lips when she colored a picture, or how her eyes lit up when her favorite cartoon came on. I couldn't remember the last time I'd been able to do that.

My vision grew misty as I wondered if she'd noticed it— my pulling away. It wasn't conscious. I would never choose anyone over my daughter. But it happened. Somehow, I'd stopped watching her like I once had. Once again, I was going to pawn her off on someone for a week.

Did she feel like I loved her less? Now that my heart was shared with Jack?

I let out an unexpected sob as I wondered what damage I'd done to my daughter. When Travis left, I promised her I'd never let anyone hurt her that way again. I'd promised it would always be me and her against the world, but so easily I'd forgotten that promise for the distraction of Jack.

RAP, RAP, RAP.

I jumped at the sudden noise, looking out my passenger window where Jack stood. I hadn't noticed him approaching the car, I was so lost in thought while watching my daughter sleep. He pulled the door open.

"What's the matter?" he asked.

I shook my head, wiping my tears dry. "Nothing, sorry. I just...had a *mom* moment." I smiled through my tears, but he climbed into the seat next to me.

"Are you sure you're okay?"

I nodded. "I just miss her."

"Miss who?" he asked, looking back at the seat where Rynlee slept.

"Rynlee."

"She's right there," he said. "What do you mean, you miss her?" He placed a hand on my shoulder, his thumb rubbing my collar bone.

"I feel like I haven't spent any time with her lately. With Meredith gone, my days are busy, my lunches are busy, and then with...you know, everything here. I just...I just miss her."

To my surprise, he didn't tell me I was being ridiculous.

Instead, he leaned in, pulling me toward him for a hug. He rubbed my back. "Hey, it's okay."

"I just feel like I'm failing at everything," I sobbed, letting out my biggest fear in one breath.

"You aren't failing at anything," he said, looking at me with shock.

"Our marriage, being a mom, running the shop, taking care of my employees...the list goes on, Jack. I can't...I can't keep up."

"So maybe *we* are failing *you*." He kissed my forehead, resting his temple on mine. "Our marriage is not failing. I love you. You're the best mom I've ever seen, including my own. Rynlee is incredibly lucky to be so loved. Have you seen the way that girl looks at you?" He pulled away, his eyes darting back and forth between mine. "Like you hung the moon, Lor. And, as far as I'm concerned, you did. Your store is beautiful, just like you, and you run it the best you can. Your employees are competent, they look up to you. You've relinquished so much responsibility to them, which is a *good* thing. That's how you lead, sweetheart. I wish I could do it as well as you." He lifted his hand, placing it on my cheek. "You are amazing. I don't know how you don't see that."

His words brought more tears to my eyes. "I love you," I said, because I couldn't say anything else. For just a moment, I closed my eyes, sinking my head into his shoulder and trying to pull myself together. "I love you so much."

"Come on inside," he said, kissing my cheek when I sat up. "I think you'll like the surprise we have for you."

"Another surprise?" I asked, raising a brow. I wasn't sure I'd survive many more of Coralee's surprises.

He opened his car door, sliding out and opening Rynlee's

door to wake her up. "Come on," he teased as he walked away from the car with Rynlee asleep on his shoulder.

When we made it inside, the house smelled of vinegar. Coralee had been cleaning.

"Should I close my eyes?" I joked, holding out a hand.

"I think you'll have trouble holding this one," Jack said with a chuckle. "Mom! She's here."

Coralee appeared from the kitchen—*why is she always doing that*—with a suitcase in her hands. *She is leaving.* Was this the surprise?

"What's this?"

"You're leaving tonight," she said, a giant grin on her face. "All three of you."

"What?" I asked, looking at Jack who was obviously in on the plan. Rynlee stirred in his arms, sitting up and looking around.

"What's going on?" she asked, letting out a yawn.

"I've packed your bags, with Jack's help, and changed your reservation. You'll be staying in a cabin with two bedrooms. There's a petting zoo down the road a bit, I've got directions in your bag. Jack said she likes animals."

My jaw dropped. "Rynlee's going?"

At the same time, Rynlee shouted, "A zoo?"

Jack smiled. "If that's what you want. We both thought it was something you would appreciate. The three of us could use some time away."

I cleared my throat. "Thank you, Coralee. You really didn't have to do this." I took the suitcase when she held it out. "I should probably check and make sure everything's here."

Jack moved toward me, placing his hand over mine. "Contacts case, pajamas, phone charger, toothbrush. It's all there. I promise. We wanted it to be all taken care of for you. I didn't want you to have to lift a finger."

Rynlee reached for me, her body falling into my arms without warning. "What do you think, kiddo? Want to go on a trip with Mommy and Jack?"

She giggled, her eyes wide with happiness. "Yes!"

"Okay," I said to Coralee, "well, I guess we'll go, then. You don't have to worry about the shop, Becky's got it taken care of. And, um, there's plenty of food in the fridge. Help yourself. Merlin's food is in the cupboard next to the fridge. He gets two cups a day."

She held up a hand to stop me, a patronizing smile on her face. "I know, Loren. I live here, too, remember? You all go. Everything will be fine, I promise." She ushered us toward the door, hugging Jack and petting Rynlee's arm.

"We'll be back in a week," I said, watching her shut the door.

"I'll see you then," she promised through the glass.

Before we could leave, I checked my bag, surprised to see that it was, in fact, packed just right. I couldn't stop looking for the setup, for the trick, the bad news to pop out. But time after time, I'd been proven wrong.

If Coralee's plan was to keep Jack and me together and happy, I'd be surprised.

If her plan was to surprise me with a setup, I'd be ready.

CHAPTER TWENTY-SIX

LOREN

"I don't think I ever want to leave," I said, groaning as Jack and I fell into bed at the end of our second night. Though I expected things to go wrong at any moment, we'd had an incredible day exploring the nearby petting zoo and local museum, and ended the evening with Jack manning the grill and Rynlee and me in the hot tub. He'd made us hot chocolate, insisting that I wasn't allowed to lift a finger or count calories all week, and Rynlee had crashed around nine-thirty.

Now, we had a whole, silent house to ourselves, and it felt like a dream come true.

"I know," he said, snaking his fingers across my arm. "What if we just never go back?"

I laughed. "Rynlee would love it. Our employees and customers would not."

"Fair enough. We could make it a tradition, though. Once a year for the rest of her childhood, we could come here. Make memories and traditions that are our own."

"Family traditions, huh?" I asked, swallowing hard as I stared at him. I took in his chiseled, scruffy jaw, his dark eyes and thick brows, the way his hair flopped over to one side when he lay down.

"It would be nice, wouldn't it? Give Rynlee something to look forward to every year. It's been a long time since I've had family traditions like that."

I ran my finger across his cheek. "It's been a long time since we've had a family."

My words caught him off guard. He sucked in a breath I didn't hear him release as he leaned forward, wrapping his arms around me and pressing his lips to mine. His kiss caused everything else to blur as I gave in to him, feeling my body melt against his. I ran a hand down his belly, feeling for his belt. His body responded to me instantly, and he pulled me on top of him, our lips never disconnecting.

It had been so long since I'd had Jack to myself. For the moment, that was all that mattered.

LIKE MOST VACATIONS, the week came to an end all too quickly. On our way home, we drove through Herrinville, the town Jack grew up in. We'd taken an agreed upon detour to prolong the trip, but also so he could point out places he'd hung out as a wild teen and the skating rink he'd bruised his knees at when he was a rambunctious ten-year-old. I wanted to know him more.

Our time away had been good for us. I felt like I was getting to know my husband on a whole new level, and my appreciation for him had grown immensely. He held my hand on the center console, his thumb grazing over my knuckles methodically.

"Hey, I have an idea," I said as we passed a familiar looking street. "What if we stop by your mother's house and clean it up a bit for her."

He gave me a quizzical look. "What? What for?"

"Well, it could only help for when she's ready to move back home. I'm sure your dad's things are still out everywhere. What if we packed a few things away for her? Made the transition a bit easier."

His thumb continued to stroke my skin. "I don't know. She might not like us going through her things."

"We won't take them anywhere. We could just pack them in boxes and move them out of her room. Or, if nothing else, just clean it up a bit. It's been empty for nearly two months. I'm sure it could use a cleaning." I squeezed his hand. "Come on, she was so nice to do this for us. I want to do something to pay her back." Jack wasn't as good as I was. He couldn't see the lie behind my innocent stare. In all reality, I wanted to get into Coralee's house to find out what I could about her. I wanted to find something to give me some insight into the enigma that she was. Jack still didn't see it. The few times I'd tried to bring up her behavior, he'd shut the conversation down quickly. I didn't want to spend the whole vacation fighting, so I'd let it go. It was for good reason, as we were now in a better place than before, but I still had a growing sense of dread as we neared our home.

Anything to put that moment off, especially something that could help me learn Coralee's dirty secrets, well, that sounded pretty appealing to me.

"I just don't know how she'll feel about us going into her house."

"You have a key, don't you?" I asked. I knew he did; it was one of only five keys on his ring—keys to the bar, the house, his car, my car, and Coralee's front door.

"I do," he confirmed with a look that said we both knew that.

"So, what could it hurt? You're her son. We'd be helping her out. Besides, aren't you ready to have our house to ourselves again? Those nights in the cabin were," I moved my hand from his, running my fingers across his forearm slowly, "so nice." I winked. "I'm not saying we rush her out, but this could be a nudge. She has to be missing home, but maybe his stuff being there just makes it that much harder to face."

He twisted his lips in thought, his eyes narrowing. Finally, he turned on his blinker and made a left at the next street. "You really think this could help her get ready to move home?"

"I do."

"Just a bit of cleaning, then," he agreed. "She hates a dusty house."

"Just a bit of cleaning," I said, looking away to conceal my grin.

A few minutes later, we pulled up in front of the old, gray home.

"It looks strange, without her in it," Jack said, staring up at the house. "Like it lost its soul or something. That sounds crazy, doesn't it?"

I shook my head. "I was thinking the same thing. Something about it looks…strange, doesn't it?"

"I guess it's just a trick of the mind." He laughed. "Let's go in, shall we?"

I moved to open my door, but stopped. "Jack, look." I pointed toward the house as a curtain swished, almost so quickly I hadn't noticed. Jack looked back to me, his eyes wide, and I knew he'd seen it, too.

Someone is inside the house.

CHAPTER TWENTY-SEVEN

LOREN

"What do we do?" Jack asked.

I tried to be rational. "Does your mother have a housekeeper?"

"Not that I know of."

"It's the middle of the day. Surely no one's broken in."

"We have to call the cops, right?"

"What if it was just a vent kicking on? What if no one's there?" I asked, thinking of his explanation about the self-closing door in Rynlee's room. "Should we call your mom?"

He stared at the dashboard, obviously trying to think through our next move. "Good idea," he said finally. "Yes, let's call and check to see if someone's supposed to be there." He pulled his phone from the holder on the dashboard, scrolling through his contacts while I kept a firm eye on the window.

"We should've been coming through and checking more often."

"More often than never, you mean?" he asked, placing the phone to his ear. "This is a safe neighborhood and the house is far enough away from its neighbors, I never thought something like this could happen." When the call connected, it beeped in through the Bluetooth, and Jack lowered it from his ear.

"Hello?" Coralee's voice called out over the line.

"Hey, Mom, it's Jack."

"What's the matter?" she asked.

"Um, okay, don't panic, but we're at your house and I'm—"

"You're what?"

"Jack," I whispered, patting his arm.

"We came by to clean up. It was supposed to be a surprise—"

"I don't need you to clean up for me, Jack. Don't worry about that. Just come on home, okay?" Her voice was urgent, and I was beginning to understand why.

"Jack," I said again, patting him harder.

"What?" he asked, looking at me as his mother continued to ramble.

"Coralee, we'll call you back," I said, pressing the end button as I nodded toward the house. Jack followed my gaze.

"What the—"

The front door of the house was opened, an East Asian man standing in the doorway with one hand over his brow to shield his eyes from the sun. Dressed in a T-shirt and jeans, he certainly didn't look the part of a burglar. A woman walked up behind him, her shiny, black hair draping over her shoulders, a daughter dressed in pink in her arms. They looked at us as we looked at them—confused.

"What should we do?" Jack asked.

"Go see who they are," I told him. Before he could budge,

the man had begun walking down the steps, then the long path, headed our way. Jack opened his door, climbing from the car, but kept his hand in the door.

"Hey, can I, um, can I help you?" the man asked, his voice wary.

"Yeah, this is kind of awkward. Do you...are you, like, *Airbnbing* or something?" Jack asked, pointing toward the house.

The man looked behind him. "Sorry, no. You could check the website, though. I'm sure someone in the neighborhood might be. Or there's a hotel just down the street. It's pretty cheap this time of year." He smiled, trying to appear friendly, but I could tell he was put off by the strange question.

Jack shook his head. "No, I'm sorry, I meant...well, this is my mother's house."

The man looked confused for a moment, then his brows raised. "Oh, wow. Man, this sucks. We never met the seller—the agent did all the work—but I didn't realize...did she pass away?"

"What? No! What seller?" Jack said, though I knew he was beginning to piece it together, same as I was.

"The seller of the house. Was it your mother's estate? Or...did she not tell you she moved?"

"T-temporarily," Jack sputtered. "She's living with my wife and I, but...are you saying she *sold* you this house?"

The man nodded cautiously. "We closed last week. I'm... really sorry if you didn't know."

Jack took a step back, the weight of what he was learning hitting him square in the gut. At the same time, I rested my head on the back of the seat, my mouth open in shock as my eyes beaded with tears.

What the hell had she done? What the hell were we going to do?

Well, I thought, as I saw Jack meet my eye, *at least you believe me now.*

CHAPTER TWENTY-EIGHT

LOREN

Coralee called over and over again for the first few minutes of our drive home, but eventually gave up, knowing her secret had been spilled. We rode in silence, both of us reeling with the revelation. What were we going to do with our newfound information?

"Surely there's some sort of explanation," Jack repeated for the fourth time.

I nodded. *There is an explanation. Your mother's a psychopath.*

We'd dropped Rynlee off with Sarah for a few hours. I knew whatever happened when we got home, it was going to be an explosion, and I didn't want her exposed to that. The bottom line was, Coralee had to leave, and if I had to call the police to get her out as a last resort, I'd hit that point pretty easily.

When we walked into the house, Coralee was sitting in the recliner, wearing a dress a shade darker than her silver hair. She wore a pearl necklace with earrings to match.

When she saw us, she leaned forward in her chair slightly,

her hands gripping the arms of the chair. She was prepared for battle.

"Mom, we need to talk," Jack began.

She nodded. "I agree."

"We met the people you sold the house to."

"Did you?" she asked, her upper lip quivering, though I saw no fear in her eyes. "I never had the pleasure. Were they nice?"

Jack stepped toward her. "Mom, what's going on? Why have you sold your house? And why didn't you tell us?"

"Were you even planning to tell us?" I demanded. "Where do you think you're going to live?"

She pushed herself up from the chair, clasping her hands at her waist with a small, sinister smile. Her voice was soft and smooth as the answer came. "Why, I'm going to live here, of course. After all, how could you kick out a frail, elderly woman? Even *you* can't be that heartless." The *you* was pointed, her gaze drilling into me.

"You're insane." I scoffed, looking at Jack. "Do you believe me now? This was her plan all along! The second she moved in here, she never planned to move out. We let her come in and get comfortable, and now she thinks she can stay." I flung a hand out toward her, begging my husband to see reason. "Jack, you have to put a stop to this. This can't go on."

He sighed through his nose, scratching his temple. "Mom, I...I don't understand. How could you—*why* would you do this? I trusted you. I went to bat for you against my wife!"

"As you well should've. I'm your mother."

"And she's my wife!" he bellowed, stepping forward so he was towering over her. "This is her house, not yours. Now, I want you to go upstairs and pack your bag. I'm going to call you an Uber."

She didn't budge. "Where, pray tell, do you propose to send me?"

"That's your own problem, created by you," he said, his eyes betraying his tone. He couldn't be nearly as harsh with her as he was trying to be. "I don't care where you go. To a hotel, to a friend's. But you can't stay here. Not after this."

She turned around, moving toward the staircase, and I held my breath. When she stopped, I let it out. I knew it wouldn't be that easy. "You know, I don't think I will be going after all." She made her way, almost floating in her dress like a ghost—no, *demon*—toward the chair she'd been in before. "And I'd like to see either of you do a thing about it."

CHAPTER TWENTY-NINE

LOREN

U p in our bedroom, while the monster-in-law lay in
wait, Jack and I paced the floors.

"What are we going to do?" I asked. "She can't stay here. I
can't handle it."

"I know," Jack said, and I could tell he was still in utter
disbelief of what had happened, as those two words were
practically all I'd managed to pull from him since we came
upstairs.

"Jack, we have to get her out of here."

"I know," he repeated.

"I'm scared of her," I told him, stopping suddenly. "I'm
scared to bring Rynlee into this house with her here."

He stopped walking, too, a scowl taking over his face.
"Oh, she wouldn't do anything to hurt her. I think this is
just...lashing out, you know? Because she feels alone. With
Dad gone, I'm all she has left."

"This isn't normal behavior, Jack. You rationalizing it
doesn't help anyone!" I screamed, panic rising in my throat.

"I'm not rationalizing it, I'm just..." He groaned. "Well,

maybe I am, but I don't know what to think, Lor. That woman down there is the same one who took care of me when I was sick and cried at my graduation. How am I supposed to accept that this is what she's become? I don't even know her anymore." His eyes were wild with fear as he said the words. "How am I supposed to move on from this? I can't kick my mother out of our home. How could I live with myself?"

I sucked in a sharp breath. "Well, you can't live with me if you don't."

He jerked his head back. "You don't mean that."

"I do, Jack. It's not fair to me or Rynlee to keep living this way. I know it's not fair to make you choose, but it's what I have to do. If you won't ask her to leave, I'll ask you both to go."

"It's my house, too," he argued halfheartedly.

"Would you really do that? Try to take my home?"

He hung his head. "No, of course not, but…"

"The choice is yours, but you don't have long to make it. If you can't get her out of here, I'm calling the police."

"Don't!" he cried. "Okay, just—just give me a minute, okay? Let me talk to her." He walked past me toward the door without another word.

I could tell he'd never forgive me for the choice I'd given him. I may have just sealed the deal on the end of our marriage on my own, but I couldn't take back what I'd said. I meant it. She had to go. *Now*. And if she took him with her, so be it.

CHAPTER THIRTY

LOREN

Coralee wasn't leaving. She'd made that abundantly clear. Jack asked me to let her sleep on it, let her realize she wasn't thinking sanely—I think he was hoping I'd do the same—but by the next morning, I was every bit as angry as I'd been the night before.

Sarah had texted me a photo of Rynlee, letting me know she was fine to stay there for a bit longer while we 'got things sorted out.' I could hear Jack and Coralee downstairs arguing, trying to make sense of our dreadful situation, but she wasn't budging. Jack would never make her.

I held the phone in my hand, the non-emergency police number on the screen. It felt drastic. I would've given anything to make any other decision, but this was what we'd come to.

I placed the phone to my ear, mentally begging Jack to forgive me. I knew it wasn't likely. I needed to save my marriage, even if that meant temporarily upsetting my husband. Coralee had sold her house. There was no way she was planning to leave now, and she'd made that clear. If we let that slide, let it be known that we knew about her sale and we'd allowed her to stay, then I wasn't sure there was any coming back from that. We had to make our stand and we had to make it now. Coralee couldn't stay in our house another moment. I wanted to cry at the thought of Jack leaving with her, of him finally choosing her over me, but I forced the thought away. He loved me. He loved Rynlee. We weren't the ones who'd lied to him.

"Little Valley Police Department, how can I direct your call?" The man sounded tired, like it'd already been a long day and I was about to make it worse.

"I, um, well…I have someone in my house that I'd like to have escorted out."

His voice became more alert when he spoke next. "Was there a break-in, ma'am?"

I hesitated. "No, not a break in. It's…it's my mother-in-law. She's been staying here, but I've asked her to leave and she won't." I felt two inches tall making the request.

There was a pause, and then the man said, "Does your husband agree with asking her to leave?"

I chose my words wisely. "We've both asked her to leave, but she's refusing."

"Okay. You mentioned she's been staying there. For how long?"

"A little over two months."

"Does she pose a threat to your safety?"

"I don't…well, I don't—"

"Has she tried to hurt you or your husband?"

"She gave my daughter cookies with peanuts. She knew she was allergic," I said, realizing all too quickly how ridiculous I must sound, how small my case against her seemed unless you'd lived it.

"She did that today? Is that why you asked her to leave?"

"No, that was about a month and a half ago." I tried to remember. "It's been a while. We've asked her to leave because…well, there have just been a lot of issues since she moved in, and it's not working out. We tried to be reasonable, but she…she just won't leave. We aren't sure what else to do."

"If you believe she was trying to harm your daughter, why didn't you ask her to leave then?"

"We weren't so sure before—"

"But you are now?"

"Yes, well, no, but—"

"Ma'am, I'm happy to take down the report for you, but I'm afraid based on what you're saying, it's something you'll have to settle amongst yourselves. We wouldn't be able to get involved unless someone was in danger."

My heart thudded in my chest. "What do you mean? It's my house."

"Did you invite your mother-in-law into your home?"

"I did, but—"

"And did you set specific ground rules for how long she could stay? Did you get it in writing?"

"Well, no, but I—"

"Unfortunately, the law doesn't see it as if she's trespassing, then. Has she paid you any rent? Helped with utilities?"

Ah, I had her there. "No, nothing."

"What about groceries? Has she contributed to your household at all? Bought any furniture?"

"She…bought wallpaper. And food, once or twice." I thought back to the meatloaf she'd surprised us with—had she known? Was it her plan all along?

He clicked his tongue. "See, all of that makes this sticky.

The law sees it as a family spat. We aren't allowed to get involved in issues like this without a court order."

"So, what are you saying? I can't make her leave *at all*? Unless she tries to hurt us?"

"There are still ways, but it gets complicated and could take months, if not years. Your best bet would be to go talk to a lawyer about your options. I believe you'd need to send her an eviction notice, via certified letter. You'll have to give her sufficient notice to find a place to stay. She'd be given a reasonable amount of time to leave. It would need to go through the courts, and it could be costly if she refuses from there. Let's hope it doesn't get to that point, though. Usually families are able to work this sort of thing out without it having to go too far." His tone was light, and he was trying to make me feel as if this could all go away with a nice sit down chat, just like Jack had, but I knew better. Coralee wasn't going to be reasoned with. I sighed.

"Sorry," he said. "I wish I had better news. If she were to try and harm you, please give us a call back. I'm afraid that's the best I can do for you, though."

"Thank you," I said, pulling the phone from my ear before both words had left my mouth. I stared straight ahead, tears beading on my eyelashes as the news made its rounds through my head. I had no power. Coralee could stay as long as she liked unless I was willing to hire a lawyer and force her out.

I sank onto the bed, covering my mouth to stifle the angry sobs. Merlin approached me from the corner of the room, resting his chin on my lap. He was trying to offer some comfort, it seemed, but it wasn't working. What on earth was I going to do? I couldn't see the way out as I listened to Jack and Coralee's continued argument down below.

Darkness filled my thoughts, its ragged fingers wrapping themselves around my mind. We had no options. None. I couldn't catch my breath as panic rose in my throat. I'd never felt so trapped, so conflicted. I loved Jack more than anything aside from Rynlee. He'd once brought so much joy into my life, but now it was hard to see past anything but Coralee. How were we ever going to get ourselves out of this mess? And would our marriage survive the carnage that was sure to ensue?

CHAPTER THIRTY-ONE

LOREN

The next week was without a doubt the worst week of my life. Jack, Rynlee, and I lived our lives alongside Coralee, with every intention of ignoring her existence. I'd told Jack what the police told me, and while he was angry that I'd made the decision without him, he was more angry that we were out of options. Neither of us had told Coralee what we'd learned, but I assumed she already knew. Maybe she'd known from the beginning.

I kept Rynlee close to me at all times and hardly slept at night, listening to every creaking noise the house made. Coralee had given up staying holed away in her room. Instead, she'd made herself comfortable front and center, always popping up in our way when we were cooking, helping herself to our food, and relaxing in the living room— television volume way too loud—so we never got a moment away from her, unless we followed her lead and holed up in our own bedroom.

I picked out Rynlee's clothes and kept her in our room, refusing to let her go anywhere alone. It didn't feel safe.

Though Coralee hadn't outright tried to hurt any of us—that I could prove, anyway—her confrontational behavior as of late had me terrified.

I worked longer hours, spending as much time away from the house as possible. Jack and I grew further and further apart, neither of us wanting to address the issue. We needed to go to a lawyer, I knew that much, but I wasn't sure I'd last another week in that house, let alone several months.

I set the plates for dinner that night, purposefully setting three places. Coralee sauntered into the room, looking at the sinkful of dirty dishes. We'd have maggots soon if someone didn't do them, but I refused. We were at an impasse. In the past week, the messes she'd made had gone untouched. Loads of laundry, dishes, and trash piled up. Coralee's end of the house had begun to reek of decay, but I refused to do it. I'd wash everything my family touched, but I wasn't her maid, and I wouldn't clean up after her any longer.

Jack believed I was going mad, I think. Every once in awhile, I'd catch him staring at me, a worried look in his eye. When I'd glance his direction, he'd look away. We hadn't so much as touched in over a week. Everything in my life had begun to center around proving a point to Coralee. Still, the truth remained—she was ruining my life, and I was pretty sure she'd set out to do just that.

Coralee grabbed a plastic cup, dumping a scoop of spaghetti into it, and pulling out one of the last clean forks from the drawer—an olive fork, way too small for spaghetti. She walked past us, not bothering to look our way. It wasn't long before the sound of our television was too loud for us to carry on a normal conversation.

Rynlee looked up at me, her eyes wide with fear, and my heart broke. I couldn't do it anymore. I couldn't do it with

Coralee, I couldn't do it with Jack. I gripped my fork, my mind blind with rage as I stormed into the living room, unsure of what I was planning until I reached the room.

I lunged forward, grabbing the television above my head and jerking it back off the wall. It didn't budge, thanks to the metal grip holding it in place. I jerked again.

"Come on!" I screamed, pulling it back. I felt like a madwoman as I jerked a final time, the TV pulling loose from its mount and crashing to the floor, taking me with it. Merlin jumped up from where he lay across the room, disturbed by the sudden interruption to his sleep. He groaned, moving toward me to investigate what had happened. I looked up at Coralee from the ground, my body pulsing with venom. "That's *enough!*"

Her sly smile sent me reeling. She clicked her tongue. "She's unstable, Jack," she said, casting her eyes to where I saw Jack and Rynlee standing. "Tell me, sweetheart, how does it feel to know you've got an insane woman for a mommy?" She pursed her lips in mock empathy.

"What is your plan? Are you really going to stay here forever?" Jack asked, positioning himself in between Coralee and Rynlee. Rynlee burst into tears, running to my side. I stood, collecting her in my arms. "You're unwelcome, Mother. We've made that incredibly clear. None of us can live this way anymore."

"There's the door," she said, waving her hand as if she were a TV show host. "As for me, I'm perfectly fine here. I always did like a little drama in my day. Things with your father grew to be *so* boring."

I wanted to scream. I wanted to yell and throw things and drag her out of my house by the throat, but I couldn't. I'd thought of changing the locks, but she never seemed to leave the house. The bottom line was, she wasn't leaving, so we would have to.

"You can't live here if we sell the house," I said, causing Jack to look over his shoulder at me.

"I don't wanna leave," Rynlee cried harder.

Coralee sat stone still, her eyes lighting up with pleasure. "I will follow you wherever you go."

"To what end, Mom? What are you gaining from this?"

"I want to be near you, son. What else is there?"

"I don't want you around," he argued. "Not like this."

"You won't be allowed to stay if we don't invite you in, and I can promise you, that'll never happen again."

She shrugged, obviously unfazed. "Do what you must, dear."

"I'll turn off the lights, the water, the power. You'll be without anything if we leave."

"Oh, no, I wouldn't do that," she mocked. "See, according to the State, I'm legally your tenant. Leaving me without electricity or water would give me the ability to sue you." I didn't know if it was true, but I didn't doubt her words. My guess was she'd looked into all of it enough to be an expert at that point.

That seemed to be the last straw for Jack. "I can't believe you're doing this to us. To my family."

"*I'm* your family, Jack." She stood from where she'd been sitting, slamming the cup from her hands down so it sloshed the spaghetti onto the cream fabric of the chair.

"Not anymore," he said, shaking his head. "Not after this. We're leaving." He looked at me. "Go pack a bag. We're leaving, and we're going to fight to get you out of here. I never want to see you again, Mom. I'll never forgive you for this."

I hurried past him, so much pride filling my heart it

nearly hurt. I rushed into Rynlee's room and grabbed her suitcase, stuffing it to the brim. I grabbed her baby book, the photos from her wall. "Get a few of your favorite toys, sweet girl. We'll come back for the rest later." I didn't tell her I wasn't sure if that was true.

Once we were done, we headed toward my bedroom, loading up my suitcase. I grabbed everything important to me: my mother's pearls, Grandmother's quilt. I had two totes and a suitcase full of things ready for Jack to load into the car when he finally appeared. He hugged us both, whispering in my ear how sorry he was.

His apologies only made me cry harder. I didn't need 'I'm sorry,' I needed solutions, but I wasn't blind enough to think they existed.

We were in a hole, and the only way to get out was to climb—blood, sweat, and tears be damned.

We loaded into the car, silent as mice, as Jack slammed the trunk. He patted the seat next to Rynlee, allowing Merlin to climb inside. The old dog seemed just as confused as we were, restlessly pacing from the floor to the seat. I didn't ask where we were going. It didn't matter. We drove away from the home, Coralee's shadow looming in the doorway letting me know she'd won once again.

I had her son—my husband—but she had my home, my memories, my legacy. The house was the only thing I'd ever owned outright, and it meant nothing to her. It was a means to an end. She wanted her son to choose her, not me.

To be honest, if it meant getting that house back, I wasn't sure I'd disagree with the terms.

Two days later, I sobbed as we listed the house with a realtor. I was pretty sure the woman thought I was deranged, crying and snotting as we signed her contract. When she asked for pictures, I gave her the few that I had, before and after shots from when I'd had the house repainted a few years back. I tried to explain our situation with Coralee gently.

"We aren't sure if she'll let the house be shown," Jack said, clearing up my puzzling explanation.

If the realtor was confused, she didn't let on. "Well, legally, you have to give your tenants sixty days notice before you could sell, so we may have to put off closing a bit, but she's legally required to let you show the house with twenty-four hours notice. You could enforce that." She nodded, agreeing with herself. "We don't have to give her a choice."

I clung to her words, hoping we could back Coralee into a corner, get her to break a rule so she could be thrown out. It was the only hope I had.

Jack and I headed back to the hotel after that. He'd offered for us to stay in the apartment above his bar, but with the loud music and crowds all hours of the night plus Coralee's ability to show up there anytime, it wasn't ideal. I needed to be somewhere that felt safe from her, even if it couldn't last. As a last resort, we'd go there, but for now, the hotel felt a bit like a sanctuary. We had a meeting with our lawyer in an hour and a half, but nothing to do in the meantime. Sarah had Rynlee again, thank God for her, we'd boarded Merlin in a nearby kennel, and Becky was working hard to get our new employee trained. Life was being held together, but only by a thread.

It felt odd, hiring someone without Meredith's approval,

but she still hadn't replied to my last text, so I decided it served her right to be left out of the loop for once.

Jack held my hand as we walked down the hotel hallway, stepping onto the elevator. It was an empty gesture, more out of what felt like habit than love, but I didn't pull away. We'd walked on eggshells around each other since the night we left the house—longer than that, really. I'd gotten what I wanted, Jack had chosen me over Coralee. I should've been happy—happier—but I felt empty. I was too upset over all that had happened. Losing my house had sent me over the edge, depression taking a firm hold on me. I couldn't make myself feel anything for him—anything for anyone, for that matter—until our situation was resolved. Feeling anything hurt too much. The elevator doors opened on our floor, and we walked off.

I wasn't sure what our marriage would look like once Coralee was out of the way. We'd never gotten a chance to explore that. I studied his face, trying to remember the way we'd been before. Before the chaos that had consumed our lives. We'd been married less than three months, and already I felt like we'd survived decades together. The man I'd married wasn't the man standing beside me now. I wasn't sure there was a way forward for us, and I hated that Coralee had done that. How could I ever look at my husband and not feel the pain he brought into my life? I hated myself for feeling the way I did. Jack had done exactly what I wanted, and yet it wasn't enough. It wasn't enough if it meant ripping my child from the only home she'd ever known. The future I'd always pictured had been in that house, the house where I was raised, and my mother before me. I couldn't imagine a future without it. But I couldn't imagine a future without Jack either. They were separate in my mind, though they'd once been one and the same. Now, I had a choice to make. Which mattered more?

Jack pressed the keycard to the door and we made our way into the stale-smelling room. I flung myself onto the bed, staring up at the ceiling with an empty mind.

That's what I felt—emptiness. Nothing.

I walked through life in a trance, just hoping and praying the madness would end soon. I didn't want to think of the irreparable damage this had caused to my daughter, my business, my mental health. I could think about that eventually, but I needed to get the source of the issues out of my house first.

She was like an infestation, a pest, chewing her way through every aspect of my life. Given enough time, she was sure to leave what was left of my existence in shreds.

Jack was texting someone, his brows drawn together in frustration when I looked over at him.

"What's wrong?" I asked. *What isn't?*

He looked up at me. "Huh? Oh, nothing. Just a shipment at the bar came in wrong. Darryl's dealing with it." He slipped his phone back into his pocket and stood. When he slid onto the bed next to me, I laid my head on his chest, his heartbeat the first comfort I'd felt in so long.

"The house will sell," he said. "And then, everything will be better."

I scoffed, cool tears trailing down the side of my face and into my hairline. I brushed them away. "You don't know that."

"You know I'm sorry, right? I'm so incredibly sorry, Lor. I hate myself for the mess I've gotten you and Rynlee in. If I could see a way to fix it, I would do it. In a heartbeat. You are all that matters to me in this world."

"I know it's not your fault," I told him, not sure if I entirely believed it. "It just...how did this happen, you know? This isn't my life. Before, my biggest worry was making sure we had enough tulips at the store or that Rynlee took a bath the night before. Now, I'm worried about the psychological damage I've inflicted on my child and whether or not I'll ever see the only home I've ever known again." I covered my face, my shoulders shaking with sobs.

"I know," he said, cradling me in his arms. "I know. God, I just can't believe what she's done. This isn't my mother. She was never like this. Growing up she was...my best friend. We've never had a relationship like most boys do with their mothers. I was always a proud Momma's boy, and now...it's like I don't even know who she is." His voice was haunted. "How could I have not seen this coming?"

"Is this all because she wants you back in her life? Is that all it is? Because she wants you to choose her over us? To leave me?"

"Maybe," he mumbled. "Is that what you want?" I uncovered my eyes, searching his face. I knew what he wanted me to say, but I wasn't sure it was the truth.

"I don't know."

He tensed immediately, which only made me cry harder. "I'm sorry, Jack. I love you, I really do. It's just..."

"Just not enough to lose everything for me—"

"It's not that simple—"

"It is!" he argued, pulling away. He sat up on the edge of the bed, his face in his palms, back to me. "It *is* that simple, Lor. I love you enough to say the rest of the world be damned. I'm giving up everything for you—my mom, who's the only family I have left, my business, which I haven't stepped foot in for days—"

"That's not fair." I propped myself up on my elbow.

He spun around, his face wild with distress. "I'm not asking it to be fair. I'm not asking life to be fair. When I fell in love with you, I decided *no matter what*, I would choose you. If I had to walk away from the rest of my life with it in flames to choose you, I would do it. Without question, without fail. Every single time."

"Look what I've given up for you, though, Jack. Look what I walked away from. My business is falling apart too, the only home I've ever known is being lived in by a stranger—"

"And I'm sorry for that, Loren. I am. But this isn't my fault, and I think you blame me for it, anyway. I stood up to her. I asked her to leave. It's not my fault the law isn't on our side. There's literally nothing I can do except get you out of there, get you and Rynlee far away from there. And that's what I've done. But it's still not right. I've still not earned your trust, or your love…" He trailed off. "If you're going to leave me anyway, you may as well get the house back."

"I never said I was going to leave you, Jack. That's honestly the last thing I want right now." The thought of splitting up in the middle of this madness, of facing it all alone, was debilitating. I loved him, that truth was at the core of who I was, but I also partially blamed him for our situation. I couldn't separate the two.

"What do you want, then?"

"I want all of this to be over. No, I want it to never have happened. I want to go back to the moment I invited her to live with us and change my mind."

He sighed, looking away. "We could go to the cabin, you know? Not the same one, but another one. Find a new place to live, away from here. Sell our businesses, sell the house, start fresh somewhere she'd never find us. We were so happy there."

I nodded. "That all sounds great. I'm just...not sure she'd ever give you up like that." I paused. "Jack, is this why you never married? Has she always been this way?"

He scoffed and shook his head. "No. That's what I'm telling you. She's never been this way. The woman we are dealing with feels like a stranger to me." He rubbed a hand over his face, inhaling sharply. "The truth is, Coralee isn't my biological mother. I don't talk about it a lot because it never mattered to me. She's the only mother I've ever known. My mom died when I was an infant, and my dad met Coralee before I'd even turned one. They always told me the truth about my real mother, but...Coralee was more of a parent to me than my dad ever was. Don't get me wrong, Dad was a good father. But Coralee...it was like she lived to be my mother. She was the type of mom who cut my sandwiches into funny shapes for school and always..." He sniffed, though I saw no tears in his eyes when he looked at me. "Always peeled my apples. She was playful and fun, always coming up with games for us to play. And when I grew out of board games and wanted to play video games instead, she learned how to play those, too." Somehow, I couldn't picture Coralee playing video games in her evening gowns, the thought too out there to visualize. "Even when I got to be a teenager, when most boys rebelled against their moms, she was always...I don't know, she was always *there* for me, ya know? She didn't spoil me, I got into trouble plenty, but she was always there to listen. I guess I just felt like I owed her somehow. She didn't have to be there for me, didn't have to do all that she's done for me—taking care of me my whole life, being there for me when my dad got sick. She didn't have to do it, but she did. She loved me at my most unlovable. I guess I just don't know when that all changed. She's not this person, Loren. I swear to you she's not. It's…I don't know if it's because she's grieving or because she feels like she's losing me. It's like someone came in and replaced my mom, and I never even got to say goodbye. I just abandoned her when she needed me the most, and I don't understand it. I don't know what the right thing is here. All I know is…that woman living in your house is not my mother."

I glanced at the clock on the nightstand between the two beds. "We should go soon if we want to make it on time. I don't want to be billed for any longer than we have to."

He nodded, standing from the bed. When I stood with him, he took hold of my shoulders, lowering his head so he could meet my eyes. "I want you to know that I'd never regret choosing you and that I'm going to do whatever it takes to fix this mess I've put us in. I promise you that."

I stood on my tiptoes, pressing my lips to his. It was brief and cold, but still the most warmth I'd felt in so long. "I know," I told him, flicking a piece of hair from my shoulder.

Whatever it takes—that was exactly what we were going to do.

AN HOUR LATER, we stood outside of the lawyer's office. It was a grand, white house near the center of town, with four large front windows, an oversized navy blue door, and four giant pillars.

"I feel like we're going to see the President," Jack tried to joke as we walked from our car and toward the porch. There was a brass plaque that displayed the business hours and our lawyer's name, Mr. May. He felt more like a calendar girl than a lawyer, but...whatever.

Jack twisted the knob and we entered the building. It was several degrees warmer than the cool air outside and carried a distinct, stale odor in the air. We walked across the hardwood floors, our footsteps echoing with each step.

Jack cleared his throat. "Um, hello?" A desk sat in the front office, but there was no one in its chair. He glanced at me with a shrug.

I was preparing to call out again when I finally heard footsteps. I walked forward, toward the doorway that led out of the foyer, and spied two slack-clad legs descending the staircase. With a few more steps, we could see his head. Balding with white hair and kind blue eyes, he smiled at us brightly and held out his hand long before he'd reached us.

"Hello, you must be my two o'clock," he glanced at his watch, "and I guess I'm late. Sorry about that. I'm Marcus May."

Jack took his hand first. "Jack Wells," he said, "and this is my wife, Loren Wells."

I shook his hand as well. It was so large, mine felt child sized in his palm.

"Nice to meet you both." He waved us down the hall and toward an office on the left, flipping on a light. The office was basically empty, a desk taking up most of the space. The desk featured a set of large law books, held together with brass bookends. A diploma and a few photographs of two children hung on his walls. He pulled out two black chairs in front of the desk, gesturing for us to sit down, then took a seat in the oversized executive chair across from us.

"So," he pulled a notebook from his desk drawer, flipping through it, "Jack, I know we spoke on the phone and you mentioned some issues with...um," he pulled his glasses up to examine the page closer, "your mom, it says here, is that right?"

Jack nodded. "She's living in our home and refuses to leave. It was originally supposed to just be for a short time, but now she's planning to stay long term and we never agreed to that. We tried to call the police, but they directed us to you."

Mr. May smiled as if he thought we were joking, looking back and forth between us. When we didn't smile back, his expression changed. "Okay, so, yeah, they're right to direct you here. Unfortunately, in cases like this, it isn't as simple as having a trespasser taken out of your home. Legally, you let your mother live there, for however long, and without a written agreement—I'm assuming you didn't have one of those?"

We shake our heads simultaneously.

"Yeah, without a written agreement in place, there's a bit more flexibility for the quote-unquote," he made air quotation marks, "tenant." He grabbed a pen and clicked the end. "So, that's the bad news. The good news is, it's not impossible. It just takes a bit of time and..." he rubbed his fingers together to indicate money. We nodded. "So, when did your mother move in exactly?"

Jack gave him the date—we'd calculated it the night before in preparation. We weren't sure we could figure it out, but after flipping back through text messages, we found it.

"So, nearly three months," Mr. May said, his eyebrows raising slightly. "Has she contributed financially to anything in your home? Given money for utilities, food, paid you anything for allowing her to stay there?"

"She's bought groceries a few times," Jack said. "Mostly for herself. And, she bought some wallpaper—"

"That she destroyed and had to replace," I added.

Mr. May nodded, scribbling down notes as we spoke. "Does your mother have money, Jack? A place to stay when she leaves your house? Does she have anyone who she could stay with?"

"I'm an only child and my father passed away shortly before Mom moved in. She has plenty of money, though. Life insurance, and then she just sold her house as well."

His eyes grew wide and he looked up at us. "Did she sell her house with the understanding that she could stay with you?"

"No," I said adamantly. "That was never the agreement. I thought weeks, maybe a month. We agreed to let her stay until she was back on her feet after losing Jack's father, that was it. She sold the house without our knowledge."

His expression was patronizing. "See, that's where we'll struggle because 'back on her feet' isn't a legal term. It could mean something different to you than her." He scratched his forehead. "And her having excess funds means she could fight us for even longer. She could drag this out."

Jack looked at me, taking my hand. "We met with a realtor this morning to sell the house. We're worried it may be our only option, albeit a last resort. But…we don't know if Coralee will let us show the house. She never leaves it."

He chuckled under his breath. "She's going to be a troublemaker, then, isn't she?" Leaning forward onto his desk, he met my eyes. "Look, I won't lie and say this will be easy, but I *can* get her out of there. As the homeowners, the law is ultimately on your side. If you decide to sell it, you only have to give her sixty days written notice. We can do that today.

She's legally required to let you show it as often as you'd like given twenty-four hours notice, but," he grimaced, "we can't force her not to be there during the showings."

I rolled my eyes, hoping and praying we could find someone to buy it sight unseen. Oakton was a seller's market, after all, and our tiny town was just an hour's drive away.

"The good news is, you've got me on your team now. We're going to handle this together." He smiled. "Now, will you be paying with cash or a check?"

CHAPTER THIRTY-TWO

LOREN

W e lived in the hotel for three more weeks before the first potential showing. Jack and I followed our lawyer's advice and overnighted a letter to Coralee, explaining that we would be there, with our realtor, a half hour early to make sure everything was in order for the showing.

It didn't say it word for word, but the fine print was there: *make yourself scarce.* Jack had tried to call her a few times, but got no answer. Eventually, we'd given up.

We drove to the house that afternoon with fear and apprehension in our bellies. It had been almost a month since we'd seen our home, and it nearly made me sick to think of what Coralee might be doing to it—in it. I had nightmares of her performing satanic rituals, smearing the walls with thick, sticky blood. So, I figured anything less than that couldn't be too bad.

Still, when we pulled into the driveway and I saw the house looked basically the same, I let out a heavy sob, breathing through my mouth to keep the tears from falling. Jack was silent, his jaw tight, as he put the car in park.

The mailbox was crammed full, the flap unable to be shut. It looked like she hadn't checked the mail a single time. Our certified letters had to be signed for, or else she might never have seen them either. We approached the house cautiously, the way you'd approach a hissing cat.

When Jack knocked on the door, I nearly lost it. Why should we have to knock at our own home?

When there was no reply, he turned the knob, pushing it open. I sucked in a deep breath, covering my mouth to conceal my screams.

"What the hell?" he cried, speaking my thoughts into existence.

The house was littered with dirty dishes, trash, and dirty clothes. The kitchen had standing water on the floor. It reeked of rot and sewage. There were boards and sawdust everywhere, walls down—she'd obviously been doing some renovating.

I gasped as Coralee entered the room, dressed in some of my best clothes—now splattered with a hideous yellow paint.

"I didn't know I was expecting company," she said.

"Coralee, what have you done?" I demanded. "This is *not* okay."

"To what were you referring, dear?"

"We have potential buyers coming here any moment. They can't see the house like this."

She clicked her tongue. "Pity, I don't think it could be cleaned up in time."

I balled my hands into fists, my body shaking with rage. Jack put a hand on my shoulder to calm me, but it had no effect. "Let's just clean up what we can."

"I won't touch this filth—"

A knock on the door interrupted us, and I turned around to see our realtor just as a mouse scurried across the floor. I squealed, jumping out. "Out! I want out!" I cried, pushing my way past Jack and out the door so I could breathe the fresh air.

The realtor, Jerrika, jumped out of my way. "What's the —" She stopped as a whiff of the air from in our home hit her. "Oh my God." She lifted her manicured nails to cover her mouth and nose. "What is that?"

"That would be our pest problem," I spat through gritted teeth. "My mother-in-law."

"I see," Jerrika responded, nodding stiffly. She seemed to contemplate the situation. "Look, I think it's best if we cancel today's showing. I can't—I can't bring people in there." Her tone was apologetic, and I nodded, though I could feel nothing but rage.

"What the hell are we supposed to do, then?" I demanded. "We can't get her out unless we sell the house, and we can't sell the house if she keeps this up. Our only option is to let her stay until we can have her legally removed?"

The realtor twisted her lips in thought. "There's one other option, but you won't like it."

"We'll do anything," Jack said, coming to stand by my side.

"We could lower the cost of the house. You don't have a mortgage on it, so you wouldn't lose money. I know it's not ideal, but we could lower it, label it as a fixer-upper, and I could try to market it to investors looking to flip it. There's a good chance it'll sell without them having to see any more than the outside pictures."

I chewed my bottom lip nervously. "This place is all I have left of my mother, my grandparents...I have so many happy memories here." I brushed away a stray tear. "I...I planned to live there until I died, then pass it on to Rynlee."

Jack touched my shoulder, leaning in to kiss my scalp. "We don't have to do this. There has to be another way."

I choked out another sob, unable to look at either of them. "There's no other way, Jack. She's won. Don't you get it? Even if we got it back, the money it would take to fix that place up after all she's done...it would ruin us."

He kissed my head again. "I'm so sorry." It was all he could say. All any of us could say. It was done. Now we just had to get out while we were still above water.

I would've preferred drowning to my next sentence. "Do whatever you have to do. Just sell it."

JERRIKA LOWERED the price from three-hundred thousand to eighty thousand the next day. It was practically giving it away. A house down the street, not nearly as nice, had sold for seven-hundred-fifty thousand just a few weeks back.

It didn't matter. I was numb. I just wanted it gone.

Rynlee and I were at the shop when Jack's number popped up on my screen.

"Hello?" I asked, passing Rynlee a daffodil to place in the arrangement we were working on.

"Hey, guess what?"

"What?" I froze. I couldn't tell if his tone was happy or scared.

"Jerrika just called. We sold the house."

I clutched my chest, feeling relief and pain all at once. "We...we what?"

"Yeah, she just got the official offer in. Full asking price, sight unseen. They're paying in cash. We still have to wait out the remainder of our sixty-day notice for Coralee, but we did it, Lor. We're free of her."

I swallowed, sinking down on the bench behind me. My hands shook as I replayed his words over and over in my head. "It's over?"

I could tell he was smiling through the phone. "It's over."

"Thank you, Jack." I wasn't sure what I was thanking him for, but I hung up the phone, still in a daze. I pulled Rynlee toward me.

"What's the matter, Momma?" she asked, running her fingers through the tears on my cheeks.

"Nothing, sweetheart," I told her, nuzzling into her shoulder. "We're going to finally be able to get a house. Isn't that exciting?" Thank God five-year-olds don't understand subtext.

She frowned. "But I like our old house."

"I do too, baby. But it's not ours anymore. Someone else is going to live there now."

"What's wrong?" Becky asked, coming around the aisle.

I smiled through my tears. "We sold the house."

Her face was solemn, not celebratory, which was exactly what I needed as she pulled me into a hug, too.

"Did you tell Meredith you were selling it?" she asked when we separated.

I shook my head. "I haven't heard back from her in a while. I don't want to bother her."

"You'd think she'd want to know, though, right?" She shrugged. "I can't believe she's been gone this long. I don't know how you put up with her flakiness."

To be honest, Meredith was the last thing on my mind. I

gave her a warning glance directed toward Rynlee. "She's family," I said firmly.

"Yeah, well, as you're learning, family isn't always all it's cracked up to be." She flipped my hair playfully, letting me know she was kidding, but it was true. "Are you going to buy a new home here?" she asked, a subject Jack and I had approached a few times but never came to a decision on.

"I honestly don't know. Our businesses are here, so it makes the most sense."

"But...?" She waited for me to go on.

"Ryn, can you go over there and finish picking up those flowers for Mommy?" I asked, nudging her toward the stack of dead tulips on the ground. She obliged, hurrying toward them, already anxious to play in the dirt surrounding them. I looked at Becky. "*But* I worry Coralee will find us if we stay here. She knows where we work, she knows what we drive. It doesn't feel safe to stay."

She nodded. "What will you do, then?"

"Sell, I guess. I'll offer Meredith the option to buy me out if she wants to keep running it alone. Or I guess I could run it from a distance and hire more employees. I don't know, honestly. I haven't thought that far ahead."

She touched my hand, offering a kind smile. "I was just asking, there's no rush to figure it all out. One step at a time, okay?"

How was it that a girl so many years younger than me seemed to be the only one who understood how I felt? That I'd come to rely on her so much?

I pulled out my phone, clicking on Meredith's name and typing out a text. Becky was right. She needed to know.

Mer, I really need you. You've gone MIA at the worst possible time. We're selling the house and moving, I can't

keep the business anymore either. I need you to call me as soon as you see this. Xx.

I sounded desperate and needy, two things I hated, but I *was* desperate and needy, so there was no use hiding it anymore.

CHAPTER THIRTY-THREE

LOREN

Six Weeks Later

J ack and I held hands, our palms sweating, in the room of the title office where we waited to meet the new owner of our home. I'd cried so hard all morning my cheeks were raw from the salt, but as we waited, I felt stronger than I expected.

I'd taken charge of my life and my circumstances. It hurt to give up the last piece of my family that I owned, but it was freeing to know I couldn't be controlled by anyone any longer. I'd set my life on fire to give myself freedom, and that was a power no one else could give me. *Cue the Eminem soundtrack as soon as we walk from the building, thank you.*

The door opened and Jack and I turned, holding our breath to see who would walk through the door. Nothing could've prepared us for the face we saw. *Smelled,* more like. I smelled her lavender and sage scent before I saw her, and I knew. *Oh, I knew.* My stomach knotted in an instant.

"Mom?" Jack stood from his chair. "What are you doing here?"

I looked her over, holding onto a shred of hope that she'd come to her senses and was coming to apologize and hand our home back to us before we made this mistake.

She smiled, her lipstick a dark maroon, and a bit of it was smudged underneath her thin lips. "I was under the impression I was here to buy a house." She looked toward our agent. "Is that not the case?"

I launched myself at her over the table, unable to control my emotions any longer. Jack grabbed hold of me, pulling me back though I struggled against him. "*You bitch!*" I spat. "You had this planned all along, didn't you?"

"Oh, yes," she admitted. "That's exactly right. From the day you two met." There was no shame in her words; she was proud of her plot.

"What do you mean...the day we met?" Jack asked, releasing me so I fell against the table. I stood, dusting myself off and looking his way. They were at a standoff, it was obvious, but I wasn't sure exactly what was happening. "You... you did this—all of this—on purpose." The look on his face said that something monumental was hitting him, though it didn't feel like that big of a revelation to me. I furrowed my brow.

"Jack?"

He turned to me, shaking his head. "There's something I haven't told you."

CHAPTER THIRTY-FOUR

JACK

Before

"Mom, are you sure you don't want something to eat? We could stop for lunch anywhere you like. My treat." I jerked Merlin's leash, trying to get him to walk alongside me.

She patted my shoulder, her eyes searching the crowd. She'd been so distracted that day, but I couldn't decide why. We stopped walking, stepping up to face the river. "That's all right, Jack. I think I'll just have a drink when we get back to the bar. My coffee from this morning still has me satisfied."

"What are you looking for?" I asked, stepping in front of her line of vision when she turned to face the crowd again.

She held up a hand to shield the sun from her eyes, regardless of the fact that she was wearing sunglasses. "Sorry, son. I know I seem a million miles away. I've been looking for one of those little book stand things, the ones they set outside of stores sometimes. I've been reading your father all of VC Andrews' work, so I try to grab one whenever I see it."

I spun around, determined to find one for her, but as far as I could see down the boardwalk—and it wasn't far, the place was packed—I didn't see any books. It was pointless to try to search for one and then search for the exact book she wanted when we could just go straight to the place we knew wouldn't let us down. "Why don't we go across town to the actual book store? They're bound to have them."

She shook her head, sighing and patting Merlin's head. "No, no, that's all right. Maybe tomorrow. I'll just wait here a while longer, enjoy the sunshine."

"It's awfully crowded," I said. "Why don't we open up the patio at the bar? We could sit there and still be in the sun, but get you away from the crowds."

She swatted my hand away when I reached to lead her. "Jack, stop fussing over me. I'm old, not dying. I'm perfectly capable of standing in a crowd. You're the one always saying downtown is safe."

"Downtown *is* safe, but that doesn't mean you're not tired. You've just gotten over the flu and traveled from Herrinville to get here. You must be exhausted."

"I traveled last night. I'm fine now. Quit worrying." She was smiling, but her tone was serious. It was time for me to drop it.

I nodded. "I just worry about you."

"It's high time you find a girl to worry about and leave your poor mother alone. What about a nice girl like that?" She gave me a wink and I scowled, following her finger to where a woman around my age was walking with a young girl. The two had identical straw-blonde hair and pretty smiles. Even from a distance, I couldn't deny she was attractive, but she was likely married with a kid in tow. So, not exactly an ideal choice to pick out of a crowd.

"I'll find someone eventually," I told her. She'd been on me to find someone new since my break up with Evelyn two years ago, but I was in no hurry to go through all that again.

When I looked up, her eyes were bright, staring across the crowd with laser focus, following the girl. Merlin nudged my leg. "Jack, why don't you go and get me a small thing of fries?" she asked, her brows raised when she looked at me. "I've decided I am hungry, on second thought."

I nodded. "Be right back."

"Oh, leave Merlin with me," she said, holding out her hand. "You know how he is about food. He'll knock it out of your hand before you can get it to me."

I handed over the leash. She was right. Try as I might, I couldn't seem to break the old dog from trying to take food from people. He wasn't ever aggressive about it, you could tell him *no* and he'd give up pretty easily, but that didn't stop him from staring at you with those sad eyes or moving toward your food every chance he got. And if you dropped it, forget about it.

"Okay, be right back." I hurried across the riverwalk when there was a break in the crowd, walking up to a burger stand. "I need to order a small fry, please."

The man nodded, taking the cash I offered and turning around to begin scooping out the food. Before he could hand it to me, I heard a scream.

"Jack!" Mom cried. I turned around just as she'd reached me. "Merlin!" She pointed. "That mom and little girl, she had ice cream. He took off after them."

"What?" I darted off in the direction she pointed me toward. "Merlin!" I yelled, cursing the dog in my head as I zoomed through the crowd, shoving my way past people. "Merlin!"

I stopped short when I saw him, nose in the ice cream on the pavement, standing in front of his latest victims. The woman stood, scooping up her daughter and pulling her from the street quickly.

"I'm so sorry," I yelled. "I'm so sorry. Did he hurt you?" I grabbed the leash that was connected to the dog's neck. "*Merlin*," I scolded, then looked up at the woman. Her palm was bleeding, the girl crying in her arms. "I'm so sorry," I apologized again. "He took off. There were some birds or something, he thought he could catch them." I couldn't stop the lie that came out of my mouth—*he wasn't after your food, you just happened to be in his way*. It was a pitiful lie, but she didn't call me out on it. "I couldn't get through the crowd to get to him in time." I took in her appearance, even as frazzled as she must be, she was beautiful. And I didn't see a ring.

CHAPTER THIRTY-FIVE

LOREN

Present Day

Jack's eyes were wild with anger as he spoke, throwing his hands in the air and clutching his scalp. He stepped back from the table, his eyes filling with sudden tears. "You...you...you planned it all, didn't you? You really did? You forced us to meet. You coached me along through the whole relationship, told me what to do, what to say. You told me when to ask her to marry me. It was all you in that...that sneaky, conniving way you have where I don't fully know that you're controlling me. But you know it." He was pacing then. "Why? Why, Mom? And *how*? How could you do this? How did you—how did you even know her? And *why*?" His knees bent with his question, the pain of it in his words. "Did you ever even care that I love her? Was this...were you trying to hurt me? Was it about money? About Dad?" He stopped, rubbing his scalp so his hair was a mess. "I don't..." His words trailed off as his eyes bounced around the room and I could see him piecing it together.

"What are you talking about? She forced us to meet? What do you mean?"

He looked at me, his eyes wide in fear as he sucked in tears. He moved his hand to cover his mouth, obviously distraught. "Loren, I...everything about our relationship, she had a hand in. She is the one who sent Merlin after you to knock you down. She is the one who told me to stop by the flower shop and ask you out that day. She told me what to say, what to ask. She...for God's sake, she helped me pick out the ring and told me how I should do it. Told me I should include Rynlee."

"You didn't—" I started to ask him so many things: *You didn't want to marry me? You didn't want to ask me out? What are you saying?* But none of the words would come out. None. I froze, turning to stare at Coralee, because only one question mattered. "Why?" I demanded through gritted teeth.

Coralee cast a glance toward the realtor and title worker, who were both pink in the face and looked petrified. "Perhaps we should take this outside," she said, her voice as calm and collected as ever. She jerked her head in the direction of the door, then pulled it open, not bothering to wait and see if we'd follow. She had us on her string, as always, and we followed her like lost puppies out the door.

When we made it to the front steps, she stopped, staring out at the large oak trees on the title company's front lawn.

Jack spoke first. "If you didn't want me to be with Loren, why did you force me to meet her?"

"Who says I didn't want you to be with Loren?" she asked, continuing to stare straight ahead. A little boy rode by on his bike, making me think of Rynlee. I so badly wanted to be with her, to go back to a time when it was just the two of us.

A time when I thought our lives weren't great and had no idea how great they truly were.

"You've done everything in your power to tear us apart. To keep me to yourself."

Coralee looked at him then, a smirk on her lips. "Don't flatter yourself, Jack. It was never about you." She looked at me. "Or you, for that matter."

"Then what?"

She inhaled deeply, crossing her arms and rubbing her palms over her biceps as if she were cold. "Son, it was always about the house."

I sucked in a breath. I'd expected her to say anything—I was prepared for literally anything—except that. "My house?"

"Mine now," she responded. "Well, soon enough, anyway."

"W-what—what could you possibly want with my house?"

"How did you even know she had the house? When we first met, you had no idea who she was." Jack shook his head.

"Oh, my dear, you don't give me any credit at all. Do you really think I'd force you into any kind of relationship if I didn't have some sort of plan? When you and *whatsherface* broke up, you were a wreck."

"What are you saying, Coralee? You knew me? How? I didn't know you."

She raised her brow, smiling at me with a grin that sent chills down my spine. "Because, my dear, we're family."

CHAPTER THIRTY-SIX

LOREN

She paused, like she wanted me to ask more, but I was still trying to remember how to breathe. What had she said? How was it possible? *It wasn't possible.* No. No. I shook my head, arguing with the voice inside.

I looked at Jack, who, much to my—relief, surprise, I couldn't decide—looked shocked as well. "What are you talking about?" he asked, his jaw locked tight.

Coralee shrugged. "Oh, Jack, I never meant to hurt you with any of this. Honestly, I didn't. But it was what needed to be done—what *had* to be done to set things right."

"What are you *talking* about?" I demanded, bending at the waist. I was sure I was going to be sick.

"My mother, like I told you before, was very ill. Her mother had dementia first, though we didn't know it was called that then. My mother was diagnosed with it at a very young age, barely forty, and we lost her pretty quickly after that. Their eldest child, my uncle, died young and my mother was the next child in line for the house—it was willed to her immediately following her brother's death, there was never a question. But, when she got sick, my grandfather changed over the will, so it would go to their youngest child—*your* grandmother. My grandfather swore to me I'd always have a place in our family's home, but when he died, it became clear that was no longer the case. *Your grandmother* made that clear."

I shook my head, unable to make sense of what she was saying. "My grandmother? I don't understand."

She rolled her eyes as if she couldn't make it any clearer. "Your great-grandparents, my grandparents, had three children: a boy, Leo, my mother, Lenora, and your grandmother, Laura. Leo was—"

"Meredith's grandfather," I said, my voice breathless with shock. It was all lining up in my head.

"Yes, that's right. He was the first in line," she continued. "But he died in the war. His only child was an infant then, younger than even your mother and I, so it willed to the next born child: my mother. When my mother got sick, the will was changed again, passed down to their third, and last, child, your grandmother, Laura. My aunt. And then, when she died, because your mother was old enough, it went to her. Then, you. But I was next in line. The house ever going to you before me was a mistake. Your mother always resented me because I was our grandfather's favorite. She did it on purpose and there was no one around to stop her." Her grin was tight and full of pain, and when she spoke next, her face barely moved. "Until now."

"Hold on, so you're saying...we're related?" Jack asked, looking at me with an upturned lip.

I grimaced as well, unsure of what to make of the discovery, but Coralee scoffed. "You're second cousins by marriage, it's hardly related and perfectly legal."

I frowned. Did that matter? Did it make it okay?

"How could you do this?" Jack asked, stepping back from the both of us. "How could you do this to me? You—you set me up."

Coralee shook her head, still refusing to look at either of us. "I needed to get *my* house back. It should've never belonged to you. You think that it holds the only memories you have left of the family you loved, but I was *born* in that house. I will *die* in that house, and I won't let anyone get in the way of that. When I die, it will go back to Jack, and so, to you, if you stay together." She looked at me then. "This was never meant to hurt either of you, though I realized early on that was inevitable. I simply wanted what was right."

"How is any of this right?" I demanded. "Don't you know what you've done, Coralee? All for a house? All for a house that you could've lived in anyway if you'd just been kind to me?"

"A house that you destroyed with your tacky wallpaper and horrible countertops. That house deserves to be restored to its former glory. Your great-grandmother would roll over in her grave if she saw her beloved bedroom any color besides yellow." She huffed. "I didn't want to live in it, Loren. I wanted to own it. I wanted my name on those papers like they should've always been. When my family shunned me after my mother's death, I was left alone with not a penny to my name. It wasn't until I met Malcolm that I had a sense of what family really was." She glanced at Jack, her eyes showing more emotion than I'd ever seen from her. "You gave me that, Jack. You showed me what love was—what families are supposed to be. After losing my grandparents and then my mother, I'd nearly forgotten what that felt like."

"This isn't love, Coralee." I felt the weight of her name on his lips, knew the line he'd just drawn. "Whatever you think this is…it's not love. You…you used me."

"You love Loren, do you not?" she demanded, and I looked at him for an answer.

"I—yes. I do."

My heart thudded in my chest. "Then, I got what I wanted while also giving you the greatest blessing," she told him. "If you decide to disown me now, you'll still have a family to turn to. This house is all that I have left."

"That's your own fault," I told her. "You could've had all of us." I wanted to scream. I wanted to attack her. I'd never felt such anger pulsing through my veins. It had seeped into my bones—the anger, the hurt, the pain. I wanted her to pay for what she'd done, but what penance would ever be enough?

"I needed to protect the house!" she screamed.

"So, what, you just…knew where she'd be that day on the riverwalk? How could you have arranged that?"

"Someone anonymous paid for our family pictures," I answered his question, the realization hitting me square in the chest. "At the studio across from where we met. It was…" I shook my head, blinking back tears as I tried to recall the memory. "It was for one day only. The note said 'Family is what you make it.' I…I thought it was Meredith who'd done it. I was struggling with the idea of family after Travis left. Rynlee had so many questions. And…I thought family portraits were such a good idea, but I'd never splurge on a studio of that caliber. Meredith knew that. She'd never admit it, though…I just—" I looked up at her, my brows drawn together. "It was you?"

She nodded slowly. "I'd kept an eye on you all your life, making sure you never sold the house, or God forbid, died and passed it on to someone else—"

"Yeah, that really would've been the worst thing about that scenario," I said sarcastically.

"But I couldn't figure out how I'd get back in there. After all, you never knew me. I was out of the house, away from that family, years before your mother had you. I couldn't just show up on your doorstep and hope you'd let me in. Then, I read a book about a family that moved into a house, it was only supposed to be for a few weeks, but they extended their stay. The owner of the house struggled so hard to get them out, and I thought...well, reality can be stranger than fiction, can't it?" She smiled. "And you and Jack were similar ages, both single, attractive. I just needed to get the two of you to meet and...when you did, I could see my plan would fall nicely into place."

"So, I guess you got what you wanted then, huh? A house over a son?" Jack asked, the pain evident in his voice. I moved toward him instinctually, wrapping my arm through his. He smiled at my touch, though it was sad, small.

"Oh, Jack," she whispered, "I never meant to hurt you. I realized not so long ago how fickle family can be. I love you, my dear, but I could never count on you not to leave me eventually. And you did, just as I suspected. You chose her over me. The house could never do that. The house and all its memories...secrets." She drew the word out like a snake. "They'll always be there for me."

"What secrets?" I demanded. My stomach was tight with knots, anger radiating through my body. None of it felt real, like it was a nightmare I couldn't wake up from.

"You know what they say, don't you? Two can keep a secret if one of them is dead," she parroted, winking at me.

"What is this? Some sort of game to you?" I asked.

"Of course it is," she said. "It's all been a game, and I'm winning."

"What do you want to do?" Jack asked, looking down at me. "I'll fight her every step of the way if that's what you want."

I hung my shoulders, watching Coralee's face light up. Something told me she would've enjoyed the fight. It was keeping her alive, giving her a reason to keep going, but I didn't have it in me. To fight for a house when my daughter needed me to fight for her instead seemed selfish. Rynlee deserved better. She deserved a mother who was all in, ready to burn down everything if it meant protecting our family.

"I guess you were right about one thing, Coralee. Family *is* what you make it, and I'm choosing to make my family far away from anything to do with you." I nodded, trying to convince myself. "I'll sign the papers. You can have it all. But the house won't make you happy. It can't love you back." I took Jack's hand. I had no idea what came next or what we were going to do, but I knew we'd figure it out together, far away from the shadow Coralee had cast over our lives.

CHAPTER THIRTY-SEVEN

CORALEE

I walked into the house—my house, *mine*—with a fresh new set of eyes. The ink was still drying on the documents, but they all knew what it said. The house was mine. The land was mine. The secrets were mine.

The sky had grown dark, there was a storm blowing in, and it had my body pulsing with electricity. So much of my life was spent on the front porch with Grandfather, watching the storms blow in on the horizon. I walked to the kitchen, stepping over the mess I'd have cleaned up soon enough, and poured myself a glass of red wine. I swirled it around, laughing to myself as I thought of what my grandfather would say if he learned I'd turned into a wine drinker. He used to say whiskey was the only alcohol worth drinking.

Of course, he didn't know how much quicker the whiskey brought back my demons.

I walked to the record player I'd removed from the attic, pulling out a record from my childhood. I blew the dust off, watching the specks float around in the dim light, before placing the record under the needle.

I heard the crackles and pops as it came to life, a sense of calm immediately settling in me. As it played, I danced around the living room and into the foyer, closing my eyes and imagining I was fifty years younger, spinning circles while the adults played their cards and smoked their cigars in a nearby room. I could nearly smell the smoke, the illusion was so real.

The memories in the house surrounded me, almost enough to cause me to choke on my tears because they came so quickly. I laughed with a full belly laugh, one that echoed my mother's—God I loved her so. I bounded up the stairs, still dancing with each step as I listened to the echoes of the music below. There was a time when this house was always filled with the music of Louis Armstrong, Bill Monroe, and Buddy Rich, and now that I had my way, I'd make sure it went out that way. My life would end surrounded by the memories of the happiest times of my life.

I could feel it creeping up on me—the end, I mean. I caught myself making the same mistakes my mother did before her sickness took over. Minor things I'd forget, tiny memories would slip away, I'd have to search deep inside my mind to remember what I'd planned to do when I entered a room. I wasn't bad, not yet. I'd put on, played it up to carry out my plan with Loren. I'd watched it so dutifully when it happened to Mother, I knew the steps and the stages. I knew how to fake it. But I wouldn't need to for much longer. I had a few more years, perhaps. Now, I could make the most of them. I wouldn't be a burden to anyone. I'd lock myself in the house, use the life insurance and money from Malcolm's house to keep me set up for the rest of my days, and cozy up with the memories. They were all I had left.

When Mother died, she always dreamed of being in this

house again—oh, how she'd cry and she'd beg—but her family was nowhere to be found. Except me. Grandfather and Grandmother were too ill and her sister, *sad excuse for one*, at least, was always too busy. Too busy to let her sister die in peace in a place that was familiar to her as her mind slowly slipped away.

I watched as my mother's mind reverted to that of her fourteen-year-old self right before my eyes, searching for a hint of familiarity in the house she'd grown up in. But, locked away in a hospital, she wasn't given the courtesy.

I'd learned from her sad end.

I wouldn't wait for what I needed.

I wouldn't ask for peace.

I demanded it.

I'd taken it with my bare hands.

I wouldn't lose my mind in some hospital. I'd lose it surrounded by the ghosts and memories of my family, in the same walls where I was brought into the world. I walked into the bedroom, the one that Loren's child had used, but that I'd been converting back to my own since they moved out. The music was faint from up there, and I only caught little notes here and there, but none of it mattered. I took another drink of my wine, setting it down on the windowsill and making my way into the closet.

I shoved all of the child's clothes to the side, clearing off the built-in bookcase. If Loren had just looked close enough, appreciated the house for all of its fine details, there was always a chance she would've discovered my secret, but she wasn't that type. Grandfather and I would spend hours taking in every tiny crack in the wall, every blemish, every intricate piece of what made this house our home.

Then again, it was a lucky thing she hadn't, or else my

story might've ended differently. Jail was no place for an ailing woman.

I grabbed hold of the built-in, jerking it back with all my strength. I'd only allowed myself to come back to the secret room once, when I needed to hide her and I'd gotten them out of the house to the cabin for the week. I couldn't risk it any other time. I'd tried to scare the little girl, to keep her out of the room so I could come down whenever I felt like I needed to be there. I'd hold my hand on the wall, breathe in the scent, and know I was just a few feet away from my darkest secrets. I'd lived for years, nearly my whole life, with the fear that each knock on the door would be the police, there to tell me I'd been caught.

But no, here I was. Everything had worked out. I no longer had to fear being caught. No one would know my secrets until I chose to share them. My heart raced with pride rather than fear. I pulled the bookshelf away from the wall, my heart thudding loud enough to drown out any hint of music below. I grabbed the hammer from the floor, lifting it to the white walls. Before I made the first hit, I ran my hands across the plaster. When I'd entered the last time, I'd made the smallest hole possible. For the most part, the plaster was still intact from all those years ago. Grandfather's hands had been the last to touch it. It pained me to destroy his masterpiece, but I needed to this time. I would never close the room off again.

I held my breath, lifting the hammer in the air and slamming it down on the plaster. I heaved, hitting and hitting, pounding and pounding, screaming and crying as the wall began to give way. When it was finally done, the plaster shattered at my feet, I pulled away the stray pieces. The smell was the same, musty and old. I'd been able to reach parts of the hidden room from the space Loren had given me upstairs. There were other entrances to the servants' quarters, so I'd been able to sit just feet from my darkest secret, but unable to reach it from that direction. This was the only entrance to the concrete room Grandfather had built. There was no other way to access it. We'd made it that way for a reason.

I smiled as I stepped into the room, breathing in the stale air.

"Hello, my darlings," I whispered, glancing over them. There, in the center of the room, lay the bodies—one wrapped in a bedsheet, the other in a black garbage bag.

I'd done it.

No one would ever be at risk of discovering the house's secrets again.

My secrets.

My skeletons in the closet…was that *too* on the nose?

CHAPTER THIRTY-EIGHT

CORALEE

Before

"**G**randfather," I said, approaching him in his study with my head hung in shame.

"What is it?" he asked, setting down his cigar and whiskey. He laid the newspaper on his desk and stood, moving toward me.

I shook my head, unable to confess my sins. When he reached me, I collapsed in his arms, my body trembling with the weight of what I'd done. He patted my head, but stopped short.

"Coralee, you're covered in blood!" He jerked me back, holding my shoulders as he looked me over. "What happened? Are you hurt?"

I began to shake my head, but stopped. "It's...it's Don." I held out my arms then, revealing the bruises I'd always done my best to keep hidden. My grandfather looked them over, his forehead wrinkling with concern.

"By God, what's he done to you?" He moved my hair off

of my neck, where I knew he'd see the fresh, purple finger-prints. He made a noise somewhere between a scoff and a grunt. "I'll kill him."

I covered my eyes, letting the sobs overtake me once again. "Come here, now," he said. "I didn't mean that. Let's get you in to see your mother and let the men take care of this, okay?"

I shook my head, a cool eel snaking up my intestines. "That won't be necessary."

"What do you—" His eyes filled with understanding then and he took a step back. "The blood is—"

I nodded, looking down at the floor, a confirmation of his half-question. "I have to turn myself in to the police. It was an accident, Grandfather. I didn't mean to. I got so scared and I just...I grabbed the nearest thing, and it was over just like that."

"Calm down, calm down," he whispered, pacing the room. He rubbed a hand over the balding place on his scalp. "Okay, where's the body?"

"At our house," I told him.

"Does anyone else know? Did you tell anyone at all?"

I shook my head stiffly. "No one."

He took hold of my shoulder, lowering himself so he could look me directly in the eye. "We're going to take care of this, Coralee. No one's going to know. You just trust me and do as I say, you hear?"

"Of course, Grandfather. Thank you." I couldn't smile, my body still filled with ice cold fear, but a small part of me felt better knowing I'd handed over a bit of my worry.

"Let's go. We have to move with haste."

A FEW HOURS LATER, we'd wrapped my husband's dead body in a bedsheet and taken him to a part of the hidden room—the old servant's quarters—that no one was allowed to enter.

I was hyperventilating, crying and shaking as we worked. *I woke up a normal person, but I'll go to bed tonight a murderer. I am a murderer. I've killed my husband. I am a widow. He is dead.* The thoughts ran through my head with a vengeance. We patched up the wall in silence, working diligently side by side. Neither of us wanted to speak of what we'd done. It was too much. No one could ever know our secret.

Grandfather had come up with a solution, the best one there was. We'd say Don left me, ran off with another woman. I'd move back in with them—my old room was still vacant, and it happened to be the only entrance to the room we were currently plastering over. We would concrete it in from the outside. No one would be able to get in anymore, and if they asked, Grandfather would explain it away with mice and mold, which was nothing close to a stretch.

He assured me that everything would be okay, but I couldn't believe it. I'd never killed anyone before that day, never watched a man's light leave his eyes. I'd always believed that was some melodramatic thing authors used to make their books seem smarter than they were, but I'd been wrong.

There was no other way to describe the phenomenon that had occurred as he slipped away from me. A dim light faded out of his dark eyes and I'd known, without checking his pulse, that he was gone.

Now, all that was left to do was to clean up our mess and move on with our lives. I was worried, my hands shaking so hard I could barely do the job I'd been tasked with.

Grandfather placed his hand on my shoulder, his soft eyes looking down at me without judgment for all I'd done.

"You've got to toughen up," he said, his words harsh despite his soft tone. "It's done. Falling apart won't change it. If we go out there and anyone sees you looking like this, they'll suspect something's happened. Go into the restroom and clean your face. I'll finish up."

I nodded. I couldn't tell if he was scolding me or trying to offer comfort. Either way, I walked across the hardwood floors of my bedroom and into the restroom across the hall.

When I glanced in the mirror, the woman looking back at me was unrecognizable. Blood was speckled across my straw-colored hair and porcelain skin.

I stuck my hands into the sink, watching the water run red. He was right, of course. I had to pull myself together.

This day had never happened. *My husband left me.* If anyone asked, I would tell them just that.

CHAPTER THIRTY-NINE

JACK

Present Day
Three Years Later

"I want to go home," Mom whined for about the fiftieth time. It was hard, listening to her wither away and knowing there was nothing I could do about it. She'd called me several times over the last few months, her mind in and out each time. I knew it was bad; we were nearing the end.

I'd tried to call the doctors for her. For my childhood, I owed her that, but she refused. She wouldn't leave the house. So, we'd settled on a private nurse checking in on her daily. The nurse came in, prepared her meals, and made sure she ate. Coralee was horrible to her. I'd had to double her salary to keep her, knowing it wouldn't be for long. According to her, Coralee didn't let her step foot outside of the kitchen or living room. She was never allowed anywhere else in the house.

I heard Coralee suck in a haggard breath. For goodbyes, it was now or never.

"You are home, Coralee," I told her, keeping my distance. "You're home."

"Why? Why? Why? Why? I want to see him. I need to see him. My Malcolm, my Malcolm. I want to go home to Malcolm," she whined, tossing and turning in her bed.

"Malcolm is dead. You don't live with him anymore," I told her. It would do no good, what I was saying to her wasn't going to click, but it was the truth nonetheless.

"I want to go home, Jack," she said again, this time using my name. It sent shockwaves through me. I was convinced she didn't know who I was anymore.

I sat down in the seat next to the bed in our room, staring at Loren. "Do you know me, Coralee? Do you know who I am?" I hadn't forgiven her. I'm not sure I ever would, but that didn't erase the memories I did have of her. Loren understood that. It's why she insisted we talk when all I wanted to do was hire a nurse.

"You're Jack," she said with a childlike lilt to her voice. "You're always Jack." I smiled at her, feeling relief.

"That's right, I'm Jack."

Her tone grew serious, deep. "Jack...I...I have something for you. Can you come to me? Can you come?" She was whispering now.

"You have something for me?" I asked, putting a finger over my other ear to make sure I was hearing her correctly.

"That's right," she whispered. "A secret. I have a secret."

I shook my head, sure she was just rambling. "Tell me, then, Coralee. What is it?" I rubbed my forehead, trying to relieve the stress.

"The house. It's yours," she said. "It should...it should stay in the family."

She seemed strangely lucid all of a sudden, but I didn't

dare be fooled by her tricks again. I swallowed, unsure of what to make of the offer. "What are you talking about, Coralee?"

"I just want to say goodbye."

"Er, goodbye then," I mumbled. Our conversations were always strange, but I couldn't help feeling like it might be my last time to say that.

"I need you to come, Jack, please. I need you to take me to my home."

"You are home," I said, but it was no use.

She cried. "Take me to Malcolm. I want to see Malcolm."

"Coralee, just...it's okay." I felt cool tears in my eyes and turned away from my wife. I didn't want her to see me break, not when I was supposed to hate Coralee. "It's okay, just calm down."

She was crying then, her sobs quiet and dainty, but I could hear them. "Come, Jack. Please. Please come. I don't want to be alone. I can't...I can't be alone."

I squeezed my eyes shut, trying to think. "Okay," I said. "Okay, I'll come. It's going to be okay."

"Yes," she whispered, her voice beginning to fade. "Yes, it'll all be...okay..."

"Goodbye, Coralee." It was the worst possible goodbye I could imagine, no real talking or chance to make amends.

"Goodbye, Jack..."

I held the phone to my ear a while longer, listening to her steady breathing. I couldn't tell if she'd completely fallen asleep, but eventually, I had to end the call. It was too painful. I wasn't sure how to feel about Coralee, about all that she'd done and all the pain she'd caused, but it didn't stop the tears from welling in my eyes at the realization that this may be my last chance to see her.

Loren approached me from behind, her soft hands wrapping around to touch my stomach. She kissed my back, resting her cheek against it.

"We can go if you want," she offered.

I groaned. "It's ridiculous. She doesn't deserve it."

I felt her nod against my skin. "No. You're right. But... maybe you deserve peace."

I lowered my hands to hers, squeezing them gently. *Peace.* It felt like a foreign concept now. Though our life had calmed considerably, I always felt like I was waiting for something to go wrong. Coralee made me feel that way.

She didn't deserve my forgiveness. Or my goodbye.

She didn't deserve any of it, yet I found myself reaching for the car keys.

CHAPTER FORTY

LOREN

We drove three hours toward Coralee's home. Jack was understandably quiet, and I wondered if he felt as nervous as I did.

I hadn't seen the house in years, not in person at least. Meredith had been keeping an eye on it, sending me texts occasionally to let me know it was still standing. She'd eloped with Billy, the boy she'd run away with, but we rotated going into town to check on the store until it eventually sold. When she did, she'd send me pictures of the house, though when it was my turn, I purposefully avoided it. I wanted to forget it existed. Forget Coralee existed.

I knew from the pictures the outside hadn't changed, but I could only imagine what she'd done to the inside. Rynlee would be in school for the next little while, so it was the perfect chance for Jack to finally get the closure he deserved, even if it pained me to do so. After today, we could walk away from our past for good.

When we pulled up to the house, I had a lump in my throat. I was terrified. What would she say? What would she do? What would she look like? It was hard to picture her frail and bedridden like Jack seemed to think she'd be.

We climbed from the car quietly, and Jack took my hand as we made our way to the porch. I studied his face, wishing I knew what he was thinking. His face was solemn, and I knew as hard as the day would be for me, I needed to be supportive. I'd be there however he needed me to be.

We reached the door with a collective inhale, and Jack put his hand on the knob. We couldn't see anything through the beveled glass, the house dark inside.

Twist.

Click.

I let out my breath as he opened the door and we stepped inside. The house was nearly unrecognizable: the walls painted a light tan, the staircase held a long, patterned runner, the floors were sanded down to a light varnish, all of my modern furniture gone and replaced with antiques.

"Mom?" Jack called into the quiet home. We ventured into the kitchen. I was shocked that my granite countertops had been replaced with green tile that ran up along the walls underneath the cabinets, which had surprisingly stayed the same. The cabinets were the only things, apparently, Coralee hadn't bothered to replace. The home looked like I'd stepped into a time capsule of her childhood, many of the furnishings identical to what I'd seen in pictures my mother had shown me.

We wandered up the stairs, noticing the changes weren't limited to the bottom floor. Some changes were minor, little furnishings here or there, and some were major—the second floor ceiling was now lined with intricate artwork. It was beautiful and classical, and though I thought it was magnificently done, I couldn't help but to be mad at the new *old* look. Some of it was what I had redone, but some of what she'd erased was redone by my mother, my grandmother. Pieces of our history had been erased to give Coralee a sense of herself again, who she'd once been.

I felt her in the home, her presence heavy like a spirit, and it was incredibly obvious that even if the house were to ever become mine again, it would never feel like my own.

We stopped at a spare bedroom, now converted to a library, and I ran my fingers along shelf after shelf—nothing from this century. It was as if Coralee had stopped living when she'd left this house, as if some huge part of her never left.

"Bella said Mom hasn't been able to make it up the stairs lately. I wonder where she could be," Jack mumbled, checking the next room.

Next, we walked across the hall toward our old bedroom. To my surprise, it was the only room that seemed untouched. Our bed, our artwork, and our clothes, were all still there. Even the carpet remained. I wondered if she'd ever stepped foot in there, other than to "borrow" my clothes the day we were supposed to show the house all those years ago, or if she'd always left it—knowing she'd return it to us one day. I pushed the thought from my mind. Jack had mentioned it, but Coralee wasn't in her right mind. And if she was, it was a trick. She'd never give the house back to us, and if she did, I wasn't sure I'd want it.

Next, I checked Rynlee's room, wondering if Coralee had left it the same as well. Instead, the room was completely different. It had been painted a creamy green, with white wooden detail along the bottom half of the wall. The curtains looked as old as the house itself. I was afraid to touch them for fear of the fabric falling to pieces. Her bed was grand, large wooden posts standing up in all four corners. The ceiling fan had been replaced with a brass chandelier that matched the dining room and foyer below. I moved toward the closet, surprised by how cold the room seemed compared to the rest of the house. When I stepped into the closet, I stopped, my eyes trying to decipher what I was seeing.

"What the—" Jack said, seeing the discovery at the same time I did. We took a step forward, then froze.

Beyond the closet was another room, a room I'd never seen before. The floors were wooden planks, the walls dark, patterned wallpaper and concrete, and there were shelves caving in on a far wall. None of that pulled my attention, though, not for long. Instead, my eyes locked on the center of the room, where my mother-in-law lay on the ground next to what appeared to be two dead bodies—one in a yellowing sheet with rust-colored splatters on it, the other wrapped in a black trash bag. She was dressed in a white nightgown, her graying hair splayed all around her on the floor. Was this a joke? I waited for her to pop up, to laugh in our faces at the cruel prank. When she didn't move, I felt a cold chill run over my body, my stomach knotting up in an instant.

I wanted to run, to bolt, but I couldn't. My feet were planted firmly on the floor, my muscles tense. I couldn't make myself move. Jack glanced at me, his eyes as wide with fear as mine were.

I searched the room with my eyes, trying to find something that would make sense of what I was seeing. Finally, I caught sight of something that caused me to convulse with fear.

"No..."

I walked forward without Jack, toward the left side of the

room, and past the unmoving bodies. I should've been scared, but outright confusion and disbelief overshadowed the fear. I picked up the blue purse where it had been discarded in the corner, running my fingers over the purple thread.

Eccentric and whimsical, just like her.

"No," I cried again, holding the purse with shaking hands. I looked toward the bodies.

"Loren, what is it?" Jack asked, taking a cautious step toward me.

I shoved past him, holding the purse with a tight grip, and darted out of the room and down the stairs, hot tears filling my eyes. I could hear him following close behind, calling my name. I reached the final floor and fell to my knees, pulling the purse's contents out. Her favorite plum lipstick, seven dollars, a lighter, and her ID. I turned it over in my hands, vomit spewing from my lips and onto the floor when I saw her face. *Meredith.*

CHAPTER FORTY-ONE

CORALEE

Before

The Day of the Wedding

Loren was the spitting image of her mother. Talking to her was the most painful thing I'd ever had to do, trying to pretend everything was okay, that I could welcome her into Jack's life with open arms.

It was his wedding day; I'd done what I'd set out to do. I just had to make it a bit longer, then I could finish out my plan. I walked through the bar, trying to remain unnoticed while Jack and Loren entertained, her hapless daughter teetering around between their legs.

"Coralee?" I heard my name and spun around, surprised that anyone there would know who I was.

The woman in front of me was tall and pale, with long, blonde hair. I smiled at her. "Sorry, do I know you?"

She cocked her head to the side, her mouth agape. When she hugged me, she smelled of cigarettes. "It's…it's Meredith. Your niece. Leo's daughter. I can't…wow, I can't believe you're here. What are you doing here? It's been what, twenty years?"

"Thirty," I clarified. "It's been thirty."

"Yeah, since I was...like ten. That's what I thought. It's so great to see you. What are you doing here?" She asked the question again, looking around the room to see who'd accompanied me.

"I, um—" I tried to think of an excuse, to piece together a reason for my sudden appearance at this wedding, but before I could, I heard Jack's voice.

"Mom!" I tried to ignore him, but his tone was insistent. "Mom!" He was growing closer.

I turned to greet him. "Just a moment, Jack, can't you see I'm talking to your guest?"

"Right, sorry. Find me when you're done. Hey, Meredith." He smiled apologetically to her before bouncing back to his new bride.

When I looked at her, her eyes were wide. "Coralee, Jack's your son?" She tapped her glass with her forefinger.

I nodded stiffly. "He is."

"Of course," she said, her voice soft. "Now it makes sense. I *knew* he looked familiar. Last time I saw him, he was just a toddler." She shook her head. "Coralee, you know that Loren is...she's Laurel's daughter."

Again, I nodded. "I do."

She gasped, her eyes zooming around the room to land on Loren. "*You let them get married?* Oh my God. How could you do that? What's she going to think when she finds out?"

I thought quickly. "I'm still trying to work out how to tell them. I didn't know until he introduced me today. She's the spitting image of her mother, but...he seems so happy."

She grimaced. "Yeah, Loren, too. I've never seen her this

happy." Pause. "But, we can't let them *stay* married. We have to tell them."

"There's no need to tell them. Jack is my son by marriage only. This little secret can stay ours," I told her.

She took a step past me, shaking her head. "No. She's my best friend. Related only by marriage or not, she deserves to know. I couldn't live with myself if I kept this from her. Loren and I don't have secrets. I should be the one to tell her. They haven't even filed the marriage certificate, it's not too late to stop this if that's what she wants."

I grabbed her arm, probably too tightly. She turned back to face me, her expression shocked. "What are you doing?"

"There's no need to cause a scene here." I couldn't let her tell. Not when I'd worked so hard to put this plan into motion. Not when I was so close. "Let's go into the back room and talk. Create a game plan."

She looked unsure. "I don't know, Coralee. She's...Loren's been through a lot. I think it would be better coming from me. I don't want to see her get hurt and, you're right, they can choose to just ignore it, but I wouldn't feel right if I didn't at least tell her what we know. You can deal with Jack however you want, but I know what Loren would want to know." She put a hand to her plum-colored lips. "She's going to be devastated."

"Look, I don't want anyone to get hurt. You're on Loren's side, I'm on Jack's. Together, we can make an awkward situation a bit better, but we have to handle things...delicately." I released her arm, ready to snatch it again if she argued.

"This is going to break her heart." She shook her head. "Oh my God, what are we going to do?"

"I have a plan," I lied. "A way to fix this so neither of them have to be hurt. Won't you just come hear me out?" She hesitated. "If you disagree after I've told you the plan, I won't stop you from telling her. But, at least do me the courtesy of hearing what I have to say."

To my relief, she nodded. "Yeah, okay." I led the way toward the back room. When she shut the door, I grabbed the nearest thing I could find—Jack's hammer—and I plunged it into her skull.

Family certainly complicates things, doesn't it?

When it was over, she lay at my feet, a thick puddle of blood surrounding her cracked skull. I panicked, grabbing a tarp and covering her body with it. I needed to think. To be rational. It had been so long since I'd killed anyone, and I'd vowed it would never happen again. But it had been necessary. A means to an end.

I tried to think like Grandfather, remember how calm he'd remained during the stressful moments that had haunted me my whole life. The fresh blood on my hands, figuratively and literally, was bringing back flashbacks of that night.

I inhaled deeply through my nose. I'd make it to the bathroom, clean myself up like before. Then, I'd insist that Jack and Loren head home, leave me to clean up. I could stash the body in the freezer for a while, keep it cold. Then, I'd bump up my plan to move into Loren's house. It had to happen sooner than later as it was the only way I'd be allowed access to the room. Her body would have to go in the secret room, too. It was the only way I could be sure it'd be hidden away for good.

I sighed, clearing my throat and brushing away my tears. This was not the time to panic. I thought about the original plan, to move in once Malcolm had passed—his doctors were predicting months if we were lucky, but I no longer had that kind of time.

It was merciful, wasn't it? He was suffering, after all. If I could end that, wouldn't he want me to? There was no chance he would live outside of his bed ever again. He would understand. Thank me for it, even. It was the right thing to do. The only thing.

I placed my hands in front of my face, bowing my head in prayer.

Forgive me, Father.

Forgive me, Malcolm.

CHAPTER FORTY-TWO

LOREN

When the police got there, I was a mess. They had us wait outside while they checked the house, but we'd told them what they'd find. Well, Jack did. I...couldn't tell them anything. Couldn't make words form. I paced, cried, cursed, vomited, and repeated. I screamed, my body shaking with anger and adrenaline as we waited.

I couldn't think straight. I was too out of it. Too lost in my own, clouded thoughts.

How had Meredith ended up there?

How was she dead?

I'd just texted her a few weeks ago. She'd sent me a picture of the house.

No.

No.

No.

No.

I vomited again, my jaw hurting from the tension. I sank into the grass, rolling over and staring up at the sky.

Blue.

Peaceful.

Unaware of the dangers of the earth it covered.

I lost myself in the wavy, windy sky, allowing my brain to settle into a comfortable, hazy place without thoughts or pain.

Somewhere in the distance, Jack was speaking. His voice was strange, underwater sounding. He was saying my name, maybe. Calling out to me.

No one's home.

No one's home.

No one's home.

No one.

No one.

No one.

No.

No.

No.

CHAPTER FORTY-THREE

LOREN

W hen I woke up next, I was back at my house—my *new* house—in bed. The room was dark, filled with a deafening silence. I sat up, scared of the voices in my head. Scared of the silence. Scared of the dark.

"Jack!" I screamed. His footsteps headed toward me in an instant, and the door swung open, the light blinding my eyes.

"Are you okay?" he asked, rushing toward my side and flipping on the lamp by the bed.

"I'm...no." No sense lying. "Was it her? Was it really her?"

His silence was a confirmation.

I sobbed, loudly and uncontrollably, and Jack held me as tight as he could through the pain.

"I love you, I'm sorry, I love you, I'm sorry." He repeated the words like a mantra, sometimes whispers, sometimes louder. He kissed my head, rubbed my hair.

"How?" I asked him, wiping my nose with the sleeve of my shirt.

"They don't know how, yet. But she'd been there...for years, Lor."

"Years?" I repeated. Since she went missing. I knew right then, we both knew the truth. My eyes burned from crying, my throat was sore from the cries. "It's all my fault."

"It's not your fault, Loren," Jack told me. "It's Coralee's fault. It's all Coralee's fault." He held me some more, rocking me back and forth.

"What day is it?" I asked. My head was so heavy, it felt like I'd been sleeping for years.

"It's the thirteenth." He told me the date, rather than the day of the week, and because of that, my eyes widened.

"I've been asleep for...a week?"

"Around that, yeah. Not the entire time. You had to go to the hospital...they sedated you. You were too upset. You've been...sleepy ever since."

"What about Coralee? She was..."

"She's dead, Lor." His words gave me more relief than I thought possible. A tiny gasp escaped my throat as I blinked, trying to process the information. "She was dead when we found her. They said she'd died a few hours before, probably around the time we got off the phone. She wanted us to...to find her there, I think. To find out her secrets." He nodded. "They found Meredith's phone in Coralee's bedroom. She'd been the one texting you. Just enough to keep you believing Meredith was alive. She didn't want you looking into her disappearance."

"I—I don't, um—" None of my thoughts made sense.

"I'm sorry, Loren. I'm the one who told her about Meredith disappearing on you. I mentioned it after you told me on our first date. I should've never said anything. She used it against you. She—"

"It's not your fault," I told him, though I didn't know if that were true. "I should've questioned more. I should've looked into it." I broke off my words in a sob, the reality of it hitting me. I'd never see Meredith again, never hear her laugh, never see her grand reveal of a new purse design. And who was going to tell Dora? She'd be devastated. *I* was devastated. The world seemed a darker place without my best friend.

I was crying without realizing it, tears streaming down my face while my mind was tormented by thoughts. "It's okay," Jack told me, holding me tight. "None of this is your fault, Lor. No matter what. It's all going to be okay."

But how was that possible? Meredith was gone. Nothing would ever be okay again. "Rynlee?"

"Rynlee's at school. She's fine."

"Does she...um, does she know?" I blinked rapidly, clearing my throat.

"No," he said, his head hung in shame. "I couldn't tell her. I'm sorry."

"It's okay. I will. I can." I squeezed his hand, my only source of comfort. "Jack, I don't want the house."

He nodded as if he expected me to say it. "I know."

"Since Coralee died, it'll go to you. To us. I don't want it. I want to sell it, burn it, whatever. I don't want to ever see it again." Panic rose in my throat, making it hard to breathe, at the thought of ever owning that place again.

"It's still being used in the investigation right now. They haven't identified the other body. But as soon as they're done, we'll list it. We never have to step foot anywhere near it again."

I nodded. I wanted the decision to give me peace, but it didn't. I wondered if I'd ever feel at peace again. What had she done to us?

"Is there anything I can get you?" he asked. "Something to drink, maybe?"

"I just want to sit for now, I think," I said, though my throat was incredibly dry.

"Loren?"

"Yeah?"

"There's one more thing."

"Okay." I braced myself for the worst.

"You don't have to open it if you don't want to, but it should be yours. It was found next to Coralee's bed." He opened up the drawer beside me and pulled out a faded envelope.

"What is it?" He placed it in my hands.

"A letter, I think. It was found in Coralee's nightstand. It's addressed to Laurel. Your mother, right?"

I nodded.

"That's what I thought. I…I don't know what to expect. I…never opened it."

He was too afraid of what it would say, just like me. Still, I opened the letter with shaking hands, dreading whatever was inside, but unable to deny my curiosity.

The paper that fell out was small, the words scratchy and nearly illegible. I gasped as I read them, the ramblings of a madwoman who believed she was in another time.

Laurel,
Game, set, match, dear cousin.
You married my son and stole my house, so I ruined your life.
The house and all its secrets will always belong to me.
I won.
If I ever see you again, you'll end up in the wall too.
You'll end up in the wall.

You'll end up in the wall.
You'll end up in the wall.
In the wall.
In the wall.
In the wall.
Wall.
Wall.
Wall.

DON'T MISS THE NEXT PSYCHOLOGICAL THRILLER FROM KIERSTEN MODGLIN

The opportunity of a lifetime may cost her life...

Read *The Dream Job* now:
https://amzn.to/3aTtyZm

ENJOYED THE MOTHER-IN-LAW?

If you enjoyed this story, please consider leaving me a quick review. It doesn't have to be long—just a few words will do. Who knows? Your review might be the thing that encourages a future reader to take a chance on my work!
To leave a review, please visit:
https://amzn.to/2I2OHUa

Let everyone know how much you loved
The Mother-in-Law on Goodreads and BookBub:
http://bit.ly/2VvuZrZ
http://bit.ly/39bfc5E

DON'T MISS THE NEXT KIERSTEN MODGLIN RELEASE!

Thank you so much for reading this story. I'd love to invite you to sign up for my mailing list and text alerts so we can be sure you don't miss my next release.

Sign up for my mailing list here:
http://eepurl.com/dhiRRv
Sign up for my text alerts here:
www.kierstenmodglinauthor.com/textalerts.html

ACKNOWLEDGMENTS

To my husband, Michael, and our daughter, CB, thank you for all you do to support and love me through the crazy experience of living with a writer. My books may not always have happy endings, but you two are mine.

To my family—Mom, Dad, Kaitie, Kortnee, Kyleigh, Granny, Papa, Nan, Pop, and so many aunts, uncles, and cousins—thank you for encouraging me from the very beginning and giving me just enough disfunction to create these crazy stories.

To my beta reader, Emerald, thank you for reading this book at its earliest stage and helping me clear away the rubble. I'm forever grateful we crossed paths.

To my editor, Sarah West, thank you for your amazing insights and for understanding my characters. Thank you for asking the hard questions and making this story what it is.

To my proofreading team at My Brother's Editor, thank you for being the final set of eyes on this book and really making it shine.

To my fans, especially the members of my Twisted

Readers fan group, thank you for always being my biggest cheerleaders. Thank you for supporting every idea I have and for always being excited about my next release. You guys are a dream come true.

And finally, to you. Thank you for purchasing this book and supporting my dream. Once upon a time, I wished for you.

ABOUT THE AUTHOR

Kiersten Modglin is an Amazon Top 30 bestselling author of psychological thrillers, a member of International Thriller Writers and the Alliance of Independent Authors, a KDP Select All-Star, and a ThrillerFix Best Psychological Thriller Award Recipient. Kiersten grew up in rural Western Kentucky with dreams of someday publishing a book or two. With more than twenty-five books published to date, Kiersten now lives in Nashville, Tennessee with her husband, daughter, and their two Boston Terriers: Cedric and Georgie. She is best known for her unpredictable psychological suspense. Kiersten's work is currently being translated into multiple languages and readers across the world refer to her as 'The Queen of Twists.' A Netflix addict, Shonda Rhimes super-fan, psychology fanatic, and indoor enthusiast, Kiersten enjoys rainy days spent with her nose in a book.

Sign up for Kiersten's newsletter here:
http://eepurl.com/b3cNFP
Sign up for text alerts from Kiersten here:

www.kierstenmodglinauthor.com/textalerts.html

www.kierstenmodglinauthor.com
www.facebook.com/kierstenmodglinauthor
www.facebook.com/groups/kmodsquad
www.twitter.com/kmodglinauthor
www.instagram.com/kierstenmodglinauthor
www.tiktok.com/@kierstenmodglinauthor
www.goodreads.com/kierstenmodglinauthor
www.bookbub.com/authors/kiersten-modglin
www.amazon.com/author/kierstenmodglin

ALSO BY KIERSTEN MODGLIN